Time Flies

H.M.Sealey & Gloria E. Sealey 2020

This is a work of fiction. Names, characters, events and incidents are either the products of the author's imagination or used in a fictitious manner. Any resemblance to actual persons, living or dead, or actual events is purely coincidental.

(With the exception of King Charles the First, Sydnam Poyntz and Gertrude and Tom Carnsew. They were real.)

This story is inspired by our family tree,

so we dedicate it to Gloria's own grandparents.

Christopher Saunders.

Joan Saunders.

John Sealey

and

Linda Sealey

All great ancestors to have.

Chapter One

The Long-Lost Princess Victoria

When Grandpa Bill died he left the messiest house I've ever seen. Even worse than Jonathan's bedroom, and my brother thinks used underpants should be kept in a pile until something grows out of them.

The first thing I notice is the smell, it's like wet dog, mixed with rotting turnips. Which is weird because Grandpa Bill never had a dog and I don't think there are any turnips anywhere, but the walls are thick with gross yellow tobacco stains that you can scrape with your fingernail, and there are piles of paper, old letters, ornaments and books on every surface. So many books.

"Well," Mum rolls up her sleeves and looks around the yucky smelling room. "Best start sorting it then. Time and tide wait for no man."

That's one of mum's weirdo expressions that she uses all the time. I'm not actually sure what it means. Mum probably isn't even sure what it means. It's just one of those sayings passed down through the generations – like that game where you sit in a circle and whisper a sentence to each-other. By the time it goes the whole way round it changes so much it's usually really funny. Like when Betty

Ross said *Miss French is the worst teacher,* and it turned into *Miss French burst open on the beach.* Though Alex Tanner probably changed it deliberately.

"Yuck." I poke something green and furry that I think used to be food on an old plate. "This is disgusting. Do I have to be here?"

"You do if you want the money for Kirkbury ComicCon."

Is she kidding? Of course I want the money for Kirkbury ComicCon, and I'll clean out a hundred manky old-people houses to get it. Kirkbury ComicCon is going to be *amazing!* I've always been too young before, but Jonathan's been three times and he says he'll take me this year if I can get the money. David Smith, star of *Timewalkers* is going to be there. Timewalkers is my absolute favourite TV show. A whole hour a week when I can pretend I'm anywhere but in a boring three-bedroom semi in a boring street with boring parents living a boring life.

My life is **boring.** Did I mention that?

"I'll sort out the newspapers or something." I mutter. Mum gives that smug *I've-won-and-you'll-do-what-you're-told* smile. Well *ha ha*. I'm only doing what I'm told for cold hard cash. So there.

I pick up an armful of newspapers from dinosaur times – or at least when mum was little - which is the same thing.

"I'll put these in the recycling." It doesn't smell as bad by the bins at least.

"Ooh, just wait a minute Vicky love." Mum picks her way over the boxes like an Olympic hurdler. "Just let me look. How old are they?"

She grabs the top paper and gets that look she sometimes gets when she sees something from her childhood. Which means I'm going to get a whole story about what things were like back in her day. Honestly, you'd think she was eighty, not forty.

"I remember her." She pokes the black-and-white photo, all excited. "She was whatshisname's wife – him with the shop on the High-Street, only it's a coffee shop now. She had a dog – little black poodle – used to follow me to school -"

That's it. Mum'll just sit in the ancient armchair and tell me stuff about her past for hours if I let her. So I sneak away while she's talking about *whatsherface and the big old orchard they turned into flats where I used to pick blackberries.*

The bedroom's worse than the lounge. It's so dusty it's like it hasn't been lived in for centuries, the curtains block out most of the light and there are still medicine bottles on the dressing-table. I push open the door and stare around. More papers. Piles and piles of them. I wonder how many forests died to fill this place with useless stuff that nobody's ever going to read again?

A funny thought hits me. All these papers, they must have meant something to Grandpa Bill. He must have kept them for a reason. I sweep my eyes around the room and suddenly find myself looking into a familiar, unpleasant face with mean little eyes and a long beard.

I shudder.

I still hate that painting. It used to terrify me when I was a little kid.

It's an old, old picture of a skinny, hunched up man in a cloak, holding a scythe, with a huge hourglass hanging from his belt. He's standing on a pile of jagged rocks, gazing out to sea. Only it looks more like he's staring straight at me. Like he *wants* something, only I don't know what. Whatever it is, he can't have it.

Old Father Time the little gold plaque at the bottom of the frame says. I never liked the expression in his eyes. I think he's hungry. I think he's just waiting for people to die.

I tear my eyes away from the picture, pick up a hand-written page and stare at it.

William Tremayne.

26th Great-Grandson of William the Conqueror.

Family Tree.

William the conqueror?

As in, 1066 and all that?

Seriously?

There are loads of names on the page, starting with Grandpa Bill and leading right back through the centuries. Elizabeth Plantagenet, William Granville, Gertrude Carnsew, John Tremayne. It's like a Wikipedia page only on paper.

"Hey mum?" I yell without moving.

"What is it sweetheart?" Her voice is muffled, like she has her head in a cupboard. Maybe she does.

"Are we related to William the Conqueror?"

"I think so. Yes."

"And you didn't tell me?" She tells me about the allotment her Great-Auntie Hilda had in the 1950s but not this? My mother's priorities are seriously mixed up.

"Goodness love, we aren't the only descendants by a long shot."

I look at the names again. How is this not interesting? *How*? History is generally pretty boring, all those famous dead people. But if some of those famous dead people are actual *relatives*? William the Conqueror is a *way* more interesting family member than Uncle Tommy. This is so cool. Like those stories where some girl finds out they're a long-lost princess.

Excited about history for the first time in my life, I gather up the papers – I can't wait 'til Mr. Hodgeman sees this at school. He'll be telling us about one of the kings and I can just casually mention – *oh yes, he's my 22nd great-grandfather.* Bow down to me, peasant.

Another thought hits me. *Castles?* Am I owed any castles? One of the Welsh ones maybe?

I knock the lid off the big biscuit tin by accident. Inside there are coins. Thousands of them. Dull, bronze and dirty silver. Like pirate treasure. I forget about being the long-lost Princess Victoria Whitburn Plantagenet of Elm Drive and scoop up a handful, running them through my fingers. They look old, not like proper money. I wonder if they're valuable?

There's a battered old watch on top of the coins with a leather strap. I pick it up and turn it over. I vaguely remember Grandpa wearing this. It has a little gold sun and moon on the face that move around through the day. I put it on my wrist and admire the way the silver moon looks at me. It's a pity its not working any more. It probably needs a battery.

There are words engraved on the back. I squint in the half-lit room and read them aloud.

Winds of Time take me away.

To the day before today.

Choose a coin to pay the fee,

And Father Time will honour thee.

Well, that's weird. It doesn't really mean anything. I choose one of the coins at random. It's small and silver and not very old. A ten-pence piece from 1985. I scoop out another. This one is so faded I can't even work out what the date was.

"I wonder what the winds of time are?" I ask myself. Which is daft, because I wouldn't have asked the question if I knew the answer, so there's no point in asking myself. "It's a dumb poem anyway." I don't *get* poetry. All those fancy rhymes. My Uncle Tommy thinks he's a poet and he wears ancient clothes and uses long, old-fashioned words.

A stray gust of wind slams a door shut somewhere in the house and makes me jump.

"Vicky!" Mum appears in the doorway. "What was that? You haven't broken anything have you?"

"It was just the wind." The coins in my hand feel oddly warm.

Mum bustles into the room and pulls the dusty curtains open. The whole house looks like it's been abandoned for years and years, but Grandpa Bill only died a month ago. "What wind?"

She notices the watch and smiles.

"That was Grandpa's. He never took it off."

Then she glances around the room and notes the painting. "Ugh. I hate that picture. Gives me the creeps." She half falls over a pile of books. "You haven't done very much."

"Neither have you. You're just looking at all the old papers." That *might* be unfair. Maybe she's done loads. But I bet she hasn't.

Mum smiles. She has a really pretty smile, for an old person. "Guilty as charged. It's like stepping back in time, coming here. My whole childhood's still in this house." She gives a funny little sigh. "All my books are here. I used to love reading, I don't get the time these days. Dad was a real hoarder, he couldn't bring himself to get rid of them. I bet all my old clothes are still here somewhere."

She wipes some dust from the mirror. "I miss him. He knew he was dying. The last thing he said to me was *the winds of time are coming to take me away*. He was very eloquent, your Grandpa. A bit like your Uncle Tommy." Then she brushes some more dust off her jeans and smiles again, but it's a sad smile. Like tears aren't very far away. "Why don't you keep the watch?"

"There're loads of old coins too."

"Oh those? He always collected them. He used to say he wanted a coin from every single year. He found quite a lot." She gazes around at the cluttered shelves, seeing the past. "I feel a bit like an archaeologist, every layer of old papers I peel back reveals a bit more history."

She sits on the bed and little puffs of dust jump around her. No *way* did Grandpa Bill sleep in this bed until last month. No way. Try ten years ago. "Your Dad says we just need to empty the old place out so we can sell it but, I don't know, it feels like there're so many memories here."

I wonder if she's going to cry again. I never know what to say when mum cries. I don't mind when it's the other way round so much. Like when AlexTanner accidentally-on-purpose dropped my new phone out of the window and I couldn't stop crying. Though that was mainly because I knew I'd have to re-play all three-hundred and twelve levels of *Animal-Crossy*. So that was angry-crying rather than sad-crying. But still. I'd really rather not be here right now.

Mum picks up a vase in the shape of a deer from the dressing-table. "I used to play with this when I was a little girl." She begins. I know the warning signs – she's about to tell me yet another long, boring story about how things were different in her day.

It's not that I'm not interested – sometimes I like hearing about the world when there was no Internet and twenty-five pence was, like, a fortune. But it's like Sundays. Once a week is fine.

The coins in my hand feel even hotter – so hot they're almost burning me. I open my fingers and look at them.

Are they *glowing*?

The wind comes from nowhere, the windows swing open with a crash and the curtains flap like flags, sending clouds of dust into the air. I screw up my eyes and feel myself blown backwards.

I expect to crash into the chest-of-drawers and probably bump my head. They're definitely just behind me, a big, ugly, dark wooden piece of furniture from about a million years ago.

But I don't hit it. I don't hit anything. Suddenly there's nothing behind me to hit. Not even a house.

Chapter Two

Getting Weirder by the Minute.

I open my eyes.

The wind's dropped a little but my hair's still flying around my face like Medusa's snakes in ancient Greek mythology. I can't feel the carpet beneath me. I can't even smell the musty, old-house smell any more.

I'm dreaming.

That's the only explanation. Strange things often happen in dreams. Like, one night, there was this glass paperweight and all these tiny animals started coming out of it and growing and growing

until my bedroom was full and there was a giraffe leaning out of the window and a rhinoceros in my bed. Dad says the real world is so boring dreams are like TV programmes in the brain to make things more exciting.

I'm still in Grandpa Bill's house – sort of – but now it's tidy and I'm hovering, mid-air, fifty centimetres above the floor. Which is much weirder than animals coming out of a paperweight.

Then, suddenly, there isn't a roof over my head. It disappears, tile by tile as I watch, leaving only empty air. The walls vanish too. It's totally weird.

Like being inside a Lego building while someone dismantles it.

Now I can only see trees and grass. Clouds move really fast across the sky which shifts from night to day as if someone's flicking a lightswitch. A flower opens, closes and dies, then opens, closes and dies again. Over and over and over.

Then it all stops. The wind drops and I fall to the ground right onto my bum with a massive **bump**.

I look up – there's an **enormous** horse right above me. Massive hooves like great big iron hammers over my head. I roll sideways and stare around.

BANG!

Gunshots make the air vibrate, and people shout from every direction – like when Jonathan puts YouTube on loudly when I'm trying to watch TV. It's so loud I want to cover my ears.

I'm in the middle of a *battle* – a real live battle. Men wearing weird clothing and helmets, leather boots squashing in the mud – more gunshots. More shouting. The ground is all churned up from the horses.

I scramble to my feet and head off towards the trees. Two guys are fighting with swords, they clash, metal on metal. One of the guys wears a huge hat with a long feather and he lunges at the other guy with the stabby end of the blade. I duck and carry on running. Even in a dream I don't want to be cut with a sword or crushed by a horse. I don't like horses. Not even unicorns.

I nearly reach the safety of the undergrowth when my foot gets stuck in the mud and I fall forwards. Somebody catches me before I hit the ground and I feel myself dragged into the bracken and trees, away from the fighting. The noise doesn't stop though. All that shouting. It's deafening.

"Only you could choose the middle of the Civil War Vicky. You could have picked a quieter year."

I look up into the face of my rescuer and find myself staring into a pair of eyes I've seen a zillion times before. My brain is thinking up some *really* crazy TV shows right now.

"Grandpa Bill?"

I stare at him, mouth open the way mum says makes me look like a dead fish. He's *dead*.

I went to the funeral. There was cake afterwards.

Maybe I'm dead? Maybe I got crushed by a big pile of his books or I banged my head really hard on the chest of drawers when I fell.

He looks like Grandpa Bill always looked, skin sagging like a deflated balloon and white hair wispy as cobwebs. Only his clothes aren't right. They're not right at all.

I'm suddenly aware the coins in my hand are so hot they're burning me, so I throw them down into the long grass.

The silver coin sits there, the queen staring up as if she's cross at being chucked away. The second coin, the really old one, fades away like smoke. I kneel down to look at the spot where it was. There's a small, black burn mark, but no coin.

"Don't lose the other one. You might need it."

"Might need what?"

"The coin." Then he scoops me up in his big, comfy arms and hugs me. "So, Vicky, you worked it out." He taps his big nose with the same long finger that played the piano so well. "You always were a clever girl."

"Worked what out?"

"How to release the winds of time." His eyes fall on the watch. "That's why I left the watch. I knew I wasn't coming back."

He passes me, stoops, and picks up the ten-pence piece. "I'm glad you realised you needed to bring this -" He begins, glancing down at the coin. Then his smile fades. "This is from 1985."

"I know."

"But you needed to bring *this* year's coin."

"I what?"

"To go back. That's how it works."

"To go back where?" This is the most bizarre conversation I've ever had. And I like to talk to other *Timewalker* fans – half of them are totally bonkers.

Grandpa Bill's eyes meet mine and he looks worried suddenly. "To take you back to your time of course."

I do my dead fish impression again. I think it comes naturally. But I don't get a chance to find out what Grandpa Bill means. There's another horrible BANG in the air so close it makes my teeth ache.

"The King's been routed." A boy crashes out of the undergrowth, red-faced from running. He wears funny clothes too, his trousers are way too short and his collar is frilly. "Cromwell's men –

hundreds of them."

He stops, panting, looking at Grandpa Bill as

though Grandpa Bill actually understands what he's

saying.

"What happened Tom?" Grandpa Bill grabs my

hand the way he used to when I was little and

begins leading me away from the battle at a sort of

fast march. I's not like he ever needed a walking-

stick or anything, but he was never this fast. He's

not even wearing trainers like me, just some

battered-looking leather boots.

"They reckon six-hundred dead on Rowton

Heath – the King retreated. General Poyntz has him

on the run."

"Where's the King now?"

We leave the trees behind and come to a dirt track that winds away through fields towards a town in the distance. The ugly sound of fighting finally starts to fade away and I can hear myself think again. The boy, Tom, pulls Grandpa Bill by the arm and I follow. I haven't got much choice.

I really, *really* want to wake up now.

"This way." Tom crosses the track – looking in all directions as if it's a busy road. Then he scampers back and crouches in the grass beside us. "Poyntz's men are everywhere. Stay quiet."

"This is *ridiculous*." I feel a bit cross now, being dragged around by dream-people. And I've got some prickly plant-bits stuck to my jeans. "This is *my* dream. I get to say where I go."

Tom turns around and glares at me. For a kid about my own age he has a really scary glare though his face is as grubby as if he's been rolling in mud. "You will be *quiet* girl!" He commands. Like I'm his pet dog barking at a car. I don't like this dream-boy. He's very, very rude.

"If we are caught we will all be tried as traitors to God and Parliament."

"Who cares. I'll wake up in a minute and eat breakfast and you and your dirty face will just fade away."

Now he looks at me like I've just eaten a dolphin. Grandpa Bill pats him on the shoulder.

"Vicky doesn't understand what's happening Tom." He says nicely.

"Of course she doesn't. She's just a girl." Tom answers in a nasty voice, before disappearing into the bracken. I'm so angry I can't even think up a good insult.

There's a tatty looking stone hut half-hidden in the bushes, all tangled with blackberries. Tom's head pops out of the undergrowth beside it and he beckons to Grandpa Bill.

The light's dim inside, there're no proper windows, just a square hole in the wall covered in ivy, and the straw on the floor smells of animal poo. I wrinkle up my nose but step inside. This is a really, *really* real dream. I scratch my hand where a nettle stung me and look at the little red bumps. I can *feel* them.

"I hid him here." Tom says is a whisper. "But we need to get him away."

Grandpa Bill pulls the door shut so the only light comes through the window. Then I realise there's someone else in the room. A tall figure hidden in the shadows.

Grandpa Bill, getting weirder by the minute, bows the way people bow in those boring costume-dramas on TV that Mum watches sometimes. The ones with the long dresses and feathery hats. And the sort of trousers very like the ones Grandpa Bill and Tom are wearing right now. My brain must remember all that from the TV shows. Clever brain.

"Your Majesty." Grandpa Bill addresses the man in the corner. "Are you injured?"

"A few scratches only." The man has a light, posh, cheerful voice. "Yet I believe my army has fared less well."

"Praise God that you yourself have come to no harm."

I giggle. I can't help it. It's funny hearing Grandpa Bill talk in such an old-fashioned way.

"Something amuses your boy?" The man asks, moving his head a little so I can see his long, black hair that reaches over both shoulders and his pointy little beard. His eyes are bright – interested – like a squirrel's.

"I'm not a boy." I correct him. He laughs.

"You wear breeches like a boy." He nods at my jeans. *Breeches?* What on earth are breeches?

"Well, I'm not."

"Then perhaps you should be at home with the other womenfolk, where you belong, not running around the forest."

Okay. That's just *rude.* I fold my arms and look at him crossly. "Shut up. You can't say stuff like that -"

"Your Majesty," Grandpa Bill interrupts me before I can finish my answer. And it was going to be a *great* answer. "Forgive my granddaughter.

Vicky, this is his gracious Majesty, King Charles."
Grandpa Bill gives me an odd look, like I should be
bowing too. Which I am *so* not doing.

"We haven't got a King." I say. "And Dad
always says the Royal family costs too much -"

That's when Grandpa Bill pulls me out of the
hut so suddenly I find myself blinking in the
daylight.

"You can't talk to the King like that." He hisses
in my ear. "People go to prison for less."

"It's only a dream." I can talk to dream-people
however I want to. They aren't real people.

"It's *not* only a dream." He snaps. Grandpa Bill
never snaps. Now he sounds as cross as Mr.
Hodgeman was the day I said World War Two

ended in 1995. There was no need for Mr. Hodgeman to react like that anyway. I got the right century after all.

"Of *course* it's a dream." I say. Though I suppose my dream-Grandpa Bill wouldn't realise he was only a dream. "You're dead and we were sorting out your house."

"And you found the family tree? And the coins?"

I nod. Dream Grandpa-Bill is very well informed. "And now my brain's turned it all into some freaky dream."

He shakes his head and holds me by both shoulders. "Vicky. This is *real*. You used one of my coins to travel back to 1645. The Winds of

Time know you're my Granddaughter so they probably thought you wanted to come."

I shrug. "I think I called them dumb." There's a funny, fluttery feeling in my stomach.

Fear.

Like before a dentist appointment, only way worse.

"You're dead." I say. I *know* he's dead. I've seen the grave.

"No. I'm not." His face breaks into the smile I recognise. "But I'm an old man, you and your mum can manage without me." He glances back towards the little hut. "I'm *useful* here. Back home I just sat in a chair and read books. Do you know how boring that is?"

"As boring as school?"

"Much more boring than school."

I consider this carefully. It's like how I felt when David Smith said he was leaving Timewalkers at the end of the new series. Like something I love is crumbling to dust. Right now, the *something I love* is my grasp on reality.

"Is this – is it *really* 1645?" That's a lot of years ago. Are there dinosaurs? Will I be eaten by a T-Rex? No, that's much longer ago. What about decent WiFi? Not that it matters. I don't have my phone with me anyway. Since the whole Alex-Tanner-throwing-my-phone-out-of-the-window-thing I'm not allowed to carry it around.

"The English Civil war."

"And that guy – in the hut? He's the King?"
That's crazy. Kings live in palaces. Everyone
knows that.

"Charles the First,"

For the first time I start to consider that this
isn't a dream.

"I just told the King of England to shut up."
Will he throw me in the tower of London for that? I
don't like London, there's too much traffic. Though
I suppose there aren't any cars in 1645.

Grandpa Bill grins. "Yes you did -"

But he never finishes that sentence. There's the
rustle of leaves and a crack of twigs being broken
by feet. The next minute there's a man facing us. A
tall man with a round helmet made of dull metal on

his head and the same sort of metal covering his chest.

I stare at him. He's pointing a gun at me. A long gun that takes two hands to hold. I've never even seen a gun in real life before.

"Don't move!" The man with the gun tells us.

So I don't.

Chapter Three

Too Weird to be Fun

"We're looking for Cavalier traitors." The man with the gun doesn't lower it. I sniff the air, it smells like fireworks. He's young, with a spotty face. He's probably only about the same age as Jonathan. I'm glad nobody ever trusted Jonathan with a gun. I don't even trust him with my stick-insect.

"My name is Will St.Aubyn." Grandpa Bill tells him, totally lying."This is my granddaughter. We're collecting firewood."

"This is no place to collect firewood old man." But he begins to lower his gun. He doesn't notice that neither of us are actually carrying any sticks. "Didn't you hear the battle?"

Grandpa Bill touches his ear and shakes his head. "I'm a little deaf these days I'm afraid."

"There was a battle." The man repeats the words. "The forces of God and parliament drove off those of the King. We took prisoners, but many fled.

Including the King himself. Have you seen anyone?"

Grandpa Bill seems to think for a few moments. "Well now. A battle you say? Maybe I did see strangers, but not here. More towards the River I think they were. There're nothing but squirrels here."

I wonder for a moment why Grandpa Bill is lying so much. Then I realise it must be to draw the man away from the King who's hiding on the other side of this wall. I wonder why he used a false name though?

The man with the gun grunts and steps towards the door. "My orders are to search everywhere."

"I remember now." Grandpa Bill clutches the man's arm suddenly, stopping him from opening the door. "I *did* see a man – a proper gentleman he looked."

"Where?"

"Now, let me think." He closes his eyes and makes such a funny, *thinking* face that I want to laugh. Only I don't. Because of the gun. "Over towards Wales he went. If you hurry you'll catch him."

The man nods, but still grabs the door-handle. "General Poyntz will send troops over the border -"

Grandpa Bill moves quickly – far more quickly than any seventy-six year old man should be able to move. He punches the man with the gun in the

face so hard I hear the crack. My Grandpa

actually *hits* someone. So much for his – *violence*

never solves anything – speech when I

accidentally-on-purpose bit Jonathan's leg that

time. And it was only a *little* bite.

I jump back as the man slumps against the door.

Then Grandpa Bill turns, his face so serious I

feel suddenly scared.

"Run Vicky." He tells me, making a grab for the

gun. But the other man is younger and stronger,

and Grandpa Bill's punch hasn't done much more

than surprise him.

"Where?"

"Carnsew Hall. Follow the road east. Ask for Gertrude Carnsew."

"But what about – you know – *him?*" I don't want to say *the King* in case that gets Grandpa into trouble.

"I'll deal with it. Just run." He manages to push the man against the wall of the hut. "The blue bedroom – the dresser. There's a coin there. It'll take you home. Now go."

"I'm a soldier fighting for God and Parliament – I'll see you in prison for this." The man wrenches his gun away from Grandpa-Bill. I back away, then turn and run, crashing through the undergrowth, searching for a road.

I hear a BANG that makes my whole body jump and I nearly stop running. What if Grandpa Bill's dead?

Again.

This is too weird to be fun now; I just want to go home.

Is Grandpa *really* fighting a man with a gun? A soldier? Just like in a story? Isn't Grandpa Bill a bit old to be the hero? David Smith is a hero in Timewalkers and he's only about thirty-five.

I find the track, all stones and churned up mud with lots of hoof-prints. East, Grandpa said. I twist my neck as I run and stare at the sky. Which way's east? Isn't the sun supposed to tell you which way's which? Only there isn't a sun, just lots of cloud and all *they* tell me is it might rain later.

Everything looks so *normal*. All the usual late summer flowers are in the hedgerows. There's nothing to say I'm standing on a patch of grass that was growing more than three-hundred and fifty years before I'm even going to be born.

"Where did you come from boy?"

I crash head-first into another man, bumping my nose on his armour. I rub my face. The man has a little beard like the King and peers at me from beneath his round helmet. I don't know what to say. It's more scary now I'm on my own without Grandpa Bill.

"I – I'm going to Carnsew Hall." I tell him.

"Are you a Carnsew?"

I don't answer. He has a thin, angry looking face. I don't like him at all. He shakes me by the shoulder.

"Are you deaf boy? I asked you a question."

"I'm not a boy." I tell him the same way I told the King. "I'm a girl."

He stares at me. I'm wearing my favourite jeans and a Timewalkers t-shirt. My hair's quite long but not as long as the King's, so maybe boys have long hair in 1645.

Then he starts to laugh.

"Well I'll be – a maid dressed as a boy." He takes my arm and pulls me along the track to where a grey horse nibbles at the grass. "I'll take you to

Carnsew Hall then. Girl." He laughs again. "I have business with Mistress Carnsew anyway."

The horse looks at us both like we're as interesting as rocks, and carries on eating. The man lifts me right up and sits me in the saddle. then he climbs on behind me. I cling on. I'm not a horsey-person. Not like most of the girls in my class. They were all into pink unicorns from being about three years old. Not me. Science-fiction and mythology. That's what I like. Medusa and the Minotaur and Hercules. When it comes to horses, I only like the winged sort.

It's very bumpy up here and we ride so fast the wind takes my breath away. I don't feel safe. I wish I had a seat-belt.

The trees whizz past until the track leads into town, I stare at the wooden-framed houses and it feels like I'm in another world. Is this what the past looked like? Where are the shops? One building has a dead pig hanging outside covered in flies which is really, *really* gross.

Finally, when I feel like I've been shaken up like a strawberry milkshake, we ride into the courtyard of a big house with ivy growing all over it. I recognise it at once. It's Sydnam Hall which is open to the public. Mum works here as a tour guide. I've visited loads because she gets free tickets.

I slip down from the horse on wobbly legs. It doesn't look very different except there aren't any signs and there's a stable where the tea-shop should be.

A tall woman in a long emerald-green dress sweeps out of the arched doors. She has a lot of blonde hair in little curls and white lace sleeves. She looks like a picture in a book.

"General Poyntz. What are you doing here?" She doesn't look very pleased to see him. I think he's got a very stupid sounding name to match his stupid beard.

"Mistress Carnsew. I'm looking for your husband."

"Thomas isn't here. I've told you that."

"I know you told me. I simply don't believe you. Thomas Carnsew is a known Royalist and an enemy of England."

"And you are only England's friend as long as you are being paid General."

He looks furious at that. "I seek to liberate this country from the tyrant on the throne. Now. Where is Thomas Carnsew?"

"I don't know."

The man gives the same sort of *I-don't-believe-you* frown that mum gives when I tell her the computer crashed right in the middle of my homework. Again. He puts his hand on my shoulder.

"This girl was looking to come here. Do you know her?"

The woman gazes at me thoughtfully. She has very blue eyes, like Grandpa Bill, and quite a nice face. For a minute she looks confused, then her eyes open really wide and she smiles.

"Of *course* I know this dear girl." She hurries up to me and kisses me on the cheek. "And how lovely to see you again. You must be so tired after your long journey." She starts to guide me into the house, then turns and gives the man a completely false smile. The sort a crocodile might give to its dinner. "Thank you *so* much for bringing her here safely General."

The General doesn't move.

"The King escaped the siege of Chester. He will come looking for a place to hide."

"You think he'd come here?"

"I think I'll wait a while and see."

The woman's smile doesn't move at all.

"Be my guest General." She says, before pushing me up the steps and in through the main doors.

It's funny; I've been in this house so many times. I know the wooden floorboards and the wobbly walls and the big oil-paintings. Visiting old houses isn't a lot of fun. but Carnsew hall has a really cool play-area in the gardens and the fudge they sell in the gift-shop is fantastic. But it's different now. Darker for a start; I suppose they don't have electric lights. But the big gallery looks sort of the same, and there isn't a roped-off area on the staircase.

The woman pulls me with her up the stairs and into a big bedroom I remember being famous because King Charles the first once slept here or something.

Oops.

Why did my brain only decide to remember that fact now?

The woman pulls the door closed behind me. The room has carved, wood-panelled walls and a four-poster bed with a blue canopy.

"Stay here." She tells me, pressing a finger to her lips. "General Poyntz is not William Tremayne's friend."

"How do you know Grandpa Bill?" I ask. It's not that I'm not grateful. I don't like the General much, and I feel sort of at home in Carnsew Hall, but I'm still so confused. It's worse than when Jonathan changed the settings on Dad's laptop to Spanish.

She nods at the watch.

"I recognised his timepiece on your wrist." She tells me. I glance down at look at it. It's working again. The second-hand is ticking away happily.

"Now wait here. I'll have food sent up. I have to

get rid of General Poyntz. I do not wish him to know my business."

She pulls the doors closed and disappears. I sit on the rather hard bed and gaze around.

I'm *really* here. I'm really in the past. It's actually quite scary so I turn and stare at the big, gold-framed painting that takes up half the wall.

Eeeek!

I give a little gasp of surprise, I know it at once. That same, miserable looking old man stares out into the world, hunting for someone to kill with his scythe. It's a *huge* version of the horrible little picture Grandpa has in his bedroom. I've looked into those eyes lots of times, but I've never seen them so detailed that I could count the little veins.

I stand up and peer at the gold plaque

underneath that's supposed to tell me who he is.

Only this plaque has more than just the usual

three words carved into the metal.

Winds of time take me away,

To the day before today.

Choose a coin to pay the fee,

And Father Time will honour thee.

Chapter Four

Then You Are All Deaf

"I don't know what the Winds of Time are, but you'd better take me home right now!"

I *know* I sound stupid, talking to thin air, but I'm tired and a bit scared and I just want to go back to where everything's normal. I glare at the words carved into the gold plaque. Whatever the Winds of Time are, I don't like them one bit.

I close my eyes and screw up my face, willing myself to feel that wind lift me off my feet like it did in Grandpa Bill's bedroom.

I *think* I feel a slight breeze. Come on. Home. Mum. Dad. Even Jonathan. Take me back.

"Begging your pardon miss, but I've brought you some supper."

I unscrew my eyes. I was concentrating so hard I didn't hear the door open. A girl wearing a white apron brings me a tray of food and puts it on the dresser. She has red hair tucked away under a little lacy cap-thing.

"Thanks."

She bobs a curtsey, like I'm the queen or something. Then she covers her face and giggles.

"What's so funny?"

She shakes her head. "I'm sorry miss, it's just – well – you do look strange. In those breeches."

I glance down at my jeans. "This is what everyone wears, where I come from."

"Even ladies?" She looks shocked.

"Yeah."

She crosses the room and pulls open a big, wooden dresser. "The mistress asked me to find you some more suitable clothing." She tells me, dragging out a long, blue dress. I *hate* dresses. You can't climb trees in dresses, they get all tangled in the branches and then mum yells when you go home with a big tear in the hem which so *totally* wasn't my fault.

I examine the dress. The material is heavy and there's no zip. How am I supposed to get it on? I turn it round, looking for some place to put my head. It's like trying to put a tent up with no instructions. The girl giggles again.

"Would you like me to help you miss?"

"I'm Vicky. Not *miss*." As I pull my jeans off something gives a really loud BEEP-BEEP from the pocket. The girl jumps like she's never heard that sort of sound before.

"Sorry. It's my Pocket Pet."

"Your *what* miss?"

I pull out a little blue plastic oval and tap the screen. It lights up and the electronic cat moves and meows really loudly. The girl jumps back in horror.

"It's a digital pet. Its not real."

"But it's moving miss. It's alive.

"It just needs feeding." I press the right buttons. "Honest, it's not alive. It's like – like a game."

"A cat in a tiny box? Be careful miss. The likes of General Poyntz will think you a witch for having such a thing."

I shove the Pocket-Pet back into my jeans and let the girl help me wriggle into the stiff fabric. If she's *that* scared of a cheap Japanese toy, what's she like if she sees a wasp? "What's your name?"

"Anne, miss."

Somebody knocks loudly on the door. Anne ignores it while she fastens the laces at the back of the dress. Velcro would be much quicker.

There's another knock, this time harder.

"Shouldn't you get the door?"

"He can wait." she tells me. And I think she smiles to herself.

The knock gets louder – and I realise it's not coming from the door at all, but the wall. Like a very loud mouse is behind the skirting-board.

Anne finishes dressing me and I wriggle in discomfort in the fitted dress. Then she runs to the wood panelling and presses a carved rose in the centre panel. To my surprise a whole extra door swings open and a familiar, and now even more grubby figure tumbles out into the room.

"Were you going to leave me in there all night Anne?" Tom, the very rude boy I met earlier emerges from a real-life secret passage. I've never seen a secret passage before, I had no idea Sydnam Hall even had one. It's not in the guidebook.

"I was helping my lady to dress." This time I giggle. I've never been called *my lady* before. Mum sometimes calls me *young lady,* but only when she's cross. *Don't you take that tone with me young lady.*

Tom looks at me, his hair is too long and hangs over his eyes, which have a mocking light in them that reminds me of Jonathan. "Well, at least she looks respectable now."

I kick my leg and the skirts move. I feel trapped and a bit stupid. "I don't care what you think." I tell him. "At least I wash my face." Actually, I haven't washed my face since last night because I was too busy reading an article on David Smith in Timewalkers magazine this morning.

Tom looks at Anne. "Is it safe?" Anne shakes her head.

"Indeed it's not, Master Tom. General Poyntz is in the parlour, with the Mistress. Where's Sir William Tremayne?"

"Arrested. He struck one of Poyntz's men to keep him from finding the King. As brave as lion he is."

Hang on.

Rewind.

Is *Sir William* Grandpa Bill?

"Grandpa Bill's been **arrested?** Like, by the police?" They can't arrest him. He's never even had a parking ticket. And how come he's suddenly a *Sir?*

Tom puts his finger over his lips and shushes me. "Hush. If Poyntz is downstairs we must be as quiet as the grave."

"But Grandpa Bill?"

"Protected the King. As is the duty of every loyal Englishman."

"So where's the King now?"

Tom turns, leans into the secret passage and gives a shrill whistle. A moment later a second figure climbs into the room. He's taller than he looked earlier, and his posh, velvet jacket is dusty.

Anne's gone white – and she curtseys so low its like someone cut her legs off.

"We can't leave you at Carnsew Hall Sire." Tom says. "Not if General Poyntz is downstairs."

"Then just go back the way you came." I say. I don't like Tom or the King. I'd rather they got arrested instead of Grandpa Bill.

"We can't. Poyntz's men are everywhere. Like ants. We were lucky to get in. They're searching the area."

We all hear footsteps on the staircase. A moment later the door swings open and Gertrude joins us. She sees the King and curtseys too. Then she spots Tom.

"Tom – thank heavens." She opens her arms and Tom hugs her the way I hug mum. "But his Majesty cannot stay here. General Poyntz has called his men. They're going to search the house."

Tom looks upset. "Again? What do they hope to find mother?"

"Your father." Gertrude says. Then she turns to me. "You shouldn't be here, I'm certain it must be a mistake. William would never bring you here to face such danger."

She turns to the big carved dresser, pulls open a drawer and takes out a small wooden box. She opens this and I see a coin glinting up from the velvet lining. She takes it and gives it to me. I'm amazed to see it's this year's coin. I mean, the *proper* year, 2020. The one I come from.

Hang on.

How can a woman in 1645 have a coin from a time that hasn't happened yet?

"You must pay the Winds of Time to take you back. And you must use the correct coin from the correct year."

I grip the coin. "You *know?* That Grandpa Bill travels in time?" I'm doing that fish impression and awful lot today, but it's not exactly normal. Normal people don't just say – *hey, I'm Bill and I like to pop back a few hundred years in time. Here, keep hold of this coin that won't exist for three-hundred and fifty years. No biggie.*

"William Tremayne indeed travels in time." She says, closing the drawer. "Forwards and backwards, backwards and forwards. The Winds of Time are very generous."

"I don't know if I like the Winds of Time very much. I didn't ask to come here."

"William didn't ask to come the first time either. But he still came to help me."

"To help you?"

"Of course. He is, after all, my great-grandson nine times removed. And families should always help each-other, shouldn't they?"

The King seems confused. "You speak of strange things Mistress. I confess I don't understand."

"Join the club." I say, before realising it probably wasn't a very respectful way of speaking to a King. Though I'm starting to understand a bit now. It's all about the coins. It must be. That's the *paying the fee* bit in the poem.

"Hurry now." Gertrude closes my hand around the coin. "Ask the Winds to take you home."

The coin feels warm just like before. Is it that easy? Travelling in time? If it is then why don't people do it accidentally? In shops or something? You go in for a bag of crisps and end up in 1994.

There must be more to it than just coins.

There are more footsteps on the stairs and a man's voice shouts loudly. "Search every room. That traitor's hiding here somewhere. I'm sure of it."

Gertrude turns and presses her back against the door. "Anne, help me. Tom, take his Majesty back into the tunnel. They cannot find him."

I don't know a lot of history, but I know enough to remember that this particular King gets his head chopped off.

"There are Poyntz's men on the other end."

"Then stay behind the panelling. I'll send Anne to tell you when it's safe to come out."

The door handle rattles, I throw my weight against it too.

"Go Tom." Gertrude tells him, her voice full of urgency. "And may God protect us all." She closes her eyes, like she's actually praying to God, rather than just saying it.

The handle rattles again and I feel someone push the door hard. But it doesn't take long for Tom and the King to Vanish behind the panel and for it to click closed. Gertrude looks at us and counts to three.

"Now." She says, and all three of us let go at the same time.

General Poyntz hurtles into the room,

crashes onto the bed and rolls off the other side.

He must have tried to shove the door open with his shoulder the moment we let go. Anne and I both try not to laugh as he lies on the floorboards.

"I'm terribly sorry. We had no idea you were there General."

The General sits up, rubbing his chin where he fell.

"Then you are all deaf Mistress Carnsew."

I roll the coin around in my fingers behind my back. Is that how it works? Was the first coin, the really faded one, from 1645? In which case, Grandpa must keep this modern coin here for when he wants to come home. Like a train ticket.

Except Grandpa Bill's meant to be dead. Does that mean he's never coming home?

General Poyntz stands up and adjusts the wide belt he wears. "I will ask you one final time Mistress Carnsew, where is your husband? He is a traitor to God and England, and I swear I will find him, and like Sir William Tremayne, he will lose his head."

Chapter Five

The Great General Sydnam Poyntz

"He said he's going to cut off

Grandpa Bill's head. I'm not eating

a meal with him."

This is *crazy*. Instead of telling General Poyntz to get out of her house or she'll chuck a bucket of water over him like any *normal* person would, Gertrude invited him and some of his soldiers to have a meal. Just like threatening to cut heads off is totally okay.

Well, I'm not sitting at the same table as him. I didn't sit at the same table as Jonathan for **three weeks** after he flushed my Barbie doll's head down the toilet and tried to replace it with an apricot. Not until he bought me a new doll with his own pocket money. And I'm not going to try to go home yet either. Not until I know Grandpa Bill is safe.

"Listen to me." Gertrude takes me aside in the kitchens which are big and full of cooking smells and bits of dead meat lying on plates that should be in the fridge. Only they don't have fridges yet. Or ice-cream. Or lemonade.

"Do you want your Grandfather to die?"

I shake my head. What kind of silly question is that? It was bad enough when I thought he died of old age. Having his head chopped off three hundred years before he was even born isn't the sort of funny family story you can tell at parties.

"Then we can't tell General Poyntz what we really think of him. We have to flatter him." I think my blank, fish-like look probably speaks volumes. She gives a little sigh. "Make him think we're on his side. If William Tremayne was arrested, Poyntz will know where he's being held. And if I don't let him search the house he'll arrest me too."

I pull at a piece of my hair like I used to when I was little. I feel like a sausage, all squashed into this dress. I pulled my jeans on underneath though. "Why's he looking for Tom's dad?"

"They have a history together – they fought in France. They were like brothers once." She looks sad for a moment. "Now they're on opposite sides in this terrible war."

So I sit at the big, white-clothed table in the dining room with Gertrude, General Poyntz and three other guys who guzzle their food like they've never seen a dead chicken before. Anne brings a bottle of wine and begins to fill their glasses. General Poyntz puts his hand over his so she can't pour it in.

"We serve God and England. Drunkenness and gluttony are sins."

Gertrude smiles that crocodile-smile again. She's really pretty and quite clever. "But surely a toast to your victory General?"

General Poyntz thinks about this for half a minute before he nods and lets Anne fill his cup. Anne winks, very briefly, at Gertrude, who raises her glass.

"To the great General Sydnam Poyntz. Champion of Rowton Moor." She says. And they all raise their glasses. Except me. I just sit and stare at my plate. Right now I'd like to Google the Civil War so I know what's going to happen.

"The King will head west, into Wales." One of the men says as he gulps his wine. "We'll follow at first light."

Poyntz shakes his head. "I don't think he got away. I think he's hiding." He looks directly at me. "Perhaps nearby. Being hidden by traitors."

I clutch the coin in my fist, my ticket back to normality. It's only warm because it's in my hand though. It's not hot like the other one felt before it disappeared. I try not to think about the King hiding in a secret passage upstairs.

Poyntz drinks some more wine and Anne fills his class again.

"What will happen to William Tremayne?" Gertrude asks, sipping her wine.

"He'll be tried as a traitor and executed. But first we'll see if he knows the whereabouts of Thomas Carnsew."

"Why's he a traitor?" I ask. I hadn't actually meant to say anything but it doesn't seem fair to kill someone just for supporting the King. Dad thinks the royal family is a waste of money but when Prince Charles came to Sydnam Hall once mum went *totally* fangirl and thought he was great. And they didn't even fight about it or anything.

Isn't it okay to believe different things? Why have a war about it?

"Everyone on the King's side is a traitor against God and England."

"Why?"

He looks at me like I'm really stupid, but I look back at him like he's really stupid too.

"Because the King will not yield to Parliament. He rules as a tyrant."

"So you want to cut his head off?" Seems a bit extreme.

Several pairs of eyes settle on me.

"Nobody has suggested executing the King girl."

"But you will – I mean – you're *going* to -"

Okay. Note to self. It's probably *not* a good idea to tell people in the past about their future.

"And do you see the future? Only witches see the future."

I close my mouth. I'm pretty sure being accused of witchcraft in 1645 wouldn't be fun. Poyntz finishes a second glass of wine.

"I hear William Tremayne has escaped your clutches before General. He's quite the dashing rogue." Gertrude changes the subject. She makes Grandpa Bill sound like Robin Hood.

Poyntz grunts. "William Tremayne won't escape Chester Gaol." He slams his glass down. "Nor will he escape execution for his crimes." He burps and lets Anne re-fill his glass. Two of the other men look like they're falling asleep.

Gertrude presses her finger against her lips and waits until General Poyntz's head nods forwards and lands on his plate. He doesn't move, just slumps there, snoring. The other men are fast asleep too.

"Oh dear." She smiles. "I do believe Anne may have accidentally given these men a sleeping potion in their wine. Tut." Then she looks at me.

"Your Grandfather is being held in Chester Gaol. You and I must get him out before General Poyntz wakes up."

Chapter Six

The Sound of My Digital Cat

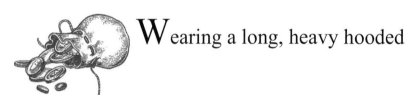Wearing a long, heavy hooded

cloak that makes me looks like Old

Father Time in the *painting*, I find myself in the

stables, in the dark. And it's really *really* dark.

Coal-mine dark. I never realised just how black the

world looks when the only lights are candles and

lanterns. The stars are really clear though, millions and millions of tiny, sparkling diamonds in the sky.

"I can't ride." I tell Gertrude as she holds the enormous animal steady. I stare into its long face with horror. It chews a mouthful of straw and looks at me like I'm the most uninteresting thing its ever seen. Hot breath snorts out of its nostrils as its jaws move up and down.

I'm not getting on *that* thing.

"You can't ride. You can't dress yourself. Is there anything you *can* do?"

I spin around to see Tom standing behind me with Anne and the King. I feel my cheeks flame red. He thinks I'm useless. Maybe now's not the time to mention that I'm *brilliant* at Animal-

Crossy. And my ability to pilot Jonathon's drone better that him probably isn't much use here either.

"I don't *need* to ride a stupid horse." I hiss. "We don't use horses. We have cars and bikes."

"Hush." Gertrude looks back towards the house. The cold night air prickles my skin and I'm suddenly grateful for the cloak. "General Poyntz and his men should sleep until dawn, but you must get his Majesty away safely."

"Is this safe?" Tom asks. He sounds nervous. I don't think he's any older than I am although I feel *much* older than eleven right now. "There are a *lot* of other soldiers out there."

"But they'll be expecting the King to be running *from* Chester, not running *to* Chester." Anne points out. I quite like Anne.

"Your maid is correct." The King says. "I can move through Chester and on into Wales. To Denbigh Castle."

"But we're getting Grandpa Bill out first, right?" I *need* Grandpa Bill. I *need* answers.

I check I still have the coin tucked away in my jeans pocket beneath my dress. I have to find out how to make the Winds of Time do their stuff, but not until Grandpa Bill's safe. I don't really care if the King gets caught. He gets his head chopped off quite soon anyway.

Gertrude brings another horse and the King climbs on so easily it's like he does it everyday, Which I suppose he does.

"I would not leave Sir William in the hands of Poyntz's dogs." The King tells us. "He has been loyal to me and I shall be loyal to him. Just as I am loyal to your husband, Mistress Carnsew."

Grandpa Bill is friends with the King? I begin to wonder how many old people sitting quietly in their houses have secrets like this. Am I totally underestimating everyone over sixty? Are they all out having adventures while I'm at school?

"Ride with Tom Vicky." Gertrude says. "Anne and I will remain here, should General Poyntz awaken. And may God go with you."

Tom climbs up to the back of his horse almost as smoothly as the King did and offers me his hand. I don't take it.

"I'm not useless." I say, suddenly determined to prove I'm not. "Okay? If you were in *my* time you couldn't do anything either." I meet Tom's eyes, they're just two, bright points in a shadowy face. He gives me a nod.

"I'm sure I couldn't." He agrees, but I think he's laughing.

I let him pull me up and I struggle in the stupid, long dress. But finally I sit behind him, holding on around his waist. The horse starts moving and my whole body jolts up and down with every step. We follow the King's horse out of the gates and onto a track that's almost invisible in the dark. I really miss streetlights right now.

"What's a car?" Tom asks as I cling on. He nudges the horse with his knees and we start moving even more quickly.

"It's like a big metal box, with seats in. And it moves by itself. You can go seventy miles an hour on the motorway."

"Seventy miles in an hour?" He seems really shocked. "The future is a wondrous place. William has often told me stories of what the world will be like."

"That's not allowed." I say. "In *Timewalkers*, they're not allowed to tell anyone *anything* about the future. Otherwise everything changes and we end up with monkeys ruling the planet." I think I might be getting mixed up with another film, but the rules for time travel are the same in every story. You don't interfere in the past. Only the bad guys do that.

He laughs as we trot along in the dark. I still don't like him, but I suppose I'm glad he's here.

"How do we rescue Grandpa Bill?" I ask. It's not like I have a time-machine like in Timewalkers. Just a coin that isn't doing anything.

"I don't know yet. Chester gaol is in the old castle. But it might not be well guarded. All the Roundheads have been laying siege to the city and fighting."

"Roundheads?"

"That's what we call Poyntz's men. Have you seen their helmets?"

General Poyntz *was* wearing a round, fitted helmet when I first met him, though I didn't take a lot of interest in his clothes at that point.

"So what's the war all about?" I ask. I know I'm going to sound really stupid but I don't have Google to ask. I miss the Internet.

For once Tom doesn't laugh at me. "The King was appointed by God to rule this country. The Roundheads think the King should bow to Parliament."

I squint ahead and see the walls of a city loom up above us. We stop in the shadows. There must be people on the walls, I can see little lights moving.

We leave our horses by the river where there's plenty of grass to graze on. In my day it's all paving slabs and a bandstand and ice-cream sellers. It feels funny to be thinking about *my day*, like Mum does. But it's odd to see a place you know really well look different. I suppose that's how it feels when you're older and you see things change.

"We will approach the castle on foot." The King says. "Sir William is known for his daring escapes."

Grandpa Bill is known for his loud farts after Sunday dinner and always winning at Top Trumps.

This Grandpa Bill is a totally different guy. Or maybe I just never knew him.

We keep to the old, sandstone walls, our hoods over our faces so we blend in with the shadows, and we creep towards the castle. I've only been here once before, to a military museum with Grandpa Bill. It wasn't very interesting. I only went for the ice-cream afterwards.

"You should stay here." The King tells me. "This is no place for a maid."

"He's *my* Grandpa." I say. "Of course I'm coming."

The King looks totally surprised. Or, at least, I *think* he'd look surprised if I could see much beneath his hood.

"Do you always answer back when told what to do girl?"

"Only when people tell me to do stupid things." Ha. He's not *my* King after all. "Anyway, I don't want to wait in the dark on my own."

"Ah. You fear the dark. Fear not maid, I will protect you."

Ugh. Do all the men here think girls can't protect themselves?

"If it wasn't for Gertrude and Anne you and Tom would still be hiding in the secret passage like a couple of rats." I say. The King chuckles.

"You have a fiery tongue girl. And bravery to equal any man. Come then. Let us save William Tremayne together." And he puts a hand on my shoulder, which, to be honest, I'm quite grateful for. I'm more scared than I'm ever going to let *him* know.

There's only one man on the door of the prison. He sits on a bench, half asleep and we crouch near the courtyard wall where we can watch him. The King puts his hand on the hilt of his sword – did I mention he's got a sword on his belt? Spiky steel that can kill someone? I don't want him to kill anyone.

"I can run this dog through." The King says.

"That's not fair." I tell him. "You don't even know him. What if he's got kids? You can't just kill people."

"You see," The King whispers to Tom, "A maid cannot understand the realities of war."

"This isn't war. That guy's just doing his job. He doesn't deserve to get stabbed for doing his job." I know in stories guards just get whacked on the head or something to get them out of the way. But this is real. And the guy dozing off on the bench is a real person.

BEEP BEEP

We all jump. My heart sinks. My Pocket-Pet decided to wait until now to tell me it wants to play. The noise is so loud it fills the whole

courtyard with the sound of my digital cat.

The guard jumps up at once and snatches up a

lantern – the old fashioned sort you get on

Christmas cards.

"Who's there?" He yells.

BEEP BEEP

I fumble in my pocket and grab the Pocket Pet,

pressing the buttons with shaking fingers and only

seeming to make it louder.

I gaze at Tom and the King – both of them look

as shocked as the guard. This is my fault. We're

going to get caught and it's all my fault.

Chapter Seven

Say The Words

"Show yourself."

BEEP BEEP

I can't shut the stupid thing off. I knew I shouldn't have bought the cheap version. But the proper one was twenty-five quid.

I didn't know the extra ten pounds would be the difference between life and death though.

The guard pulls a gun off his shoulder.

"He has a musket." I hear the King whisper a warning in my ear and hear the SNICK sound as he draws his sword. Tom tries to pull me away from the fight we know is about to happen, but I *can't* let them fight. What if the King gets shot? The history books will all change. Maybe I'll go back home and find the monkeys have taken over.

BEEP BEEP

That stupid Pocket-Pet. I'm going to starve it, I swear I am.

Then I have an idea.

I step out in front on the guard. He holds up the lantern so he can see me properly.

"Who're you?" He demands, jabbing his gun in my direction. He wears a round helmet too, although his is falling sideways over one eye.

I hold out the Pocket Pet on the palm of my hand. The little cat is jumping around, meowing loudly.

"Behold!" I use my most confident voice. "I am a great sorceress. See the cat I have trapped in my magic egg."

I press a button and the cat dances to music. The man draws back.

"What in God's name is it?"

"This is where I put all those who displease me."
I sound like a pantomime wicked queen. "Shall I
put thee in here too?" I'm really pleased with that.
Thee is old-fashioned speak for *you.*

"What trickery is this?"

Now he aims the gun at me.

Uh oh. Maybe this wasn't such a good plan.

"She has the King of England himself trapped in
her magic egg." Suddenly Tom's at my side and we
face the gun together, he slips his fingers into mine
and squeezes. The man looks at us both with
suspicious eyes.

"Hogwash. No man could fit in such a tiny box."

"Your Majesty?" Tom leans over my Pocket Pet.
The cat is now licking itself and purring. "If thou

art in the magic egg, speak now and let this man know his own terrible fate."

We wait a moment, then the King's voice echoes around the courtyard.

"Indeed these children speak the truth. I am Charles. King of England, Scotland and Ireland by the grace of Almighty God."

The guard's eyes widen in terror and he backs away, dropping his gun onto the cobblestones.

"'Tis witchcraft." He whispers, before stumbling, turning, and then running away.

Tom collapses in laughter. "Oh – oh – that was a grand jest. Did you see his face. He couldn't have been more afraid had the hoards of Hell ridden forth."

The King steps out of the shadows and claps Tom on the back.

"Indeed. The maid has a clever mind." And the King actually gives me a little bow, taking off his big, plumed hat. Tom grins at me, and all at once I don't feel so useless. I turn the Pocket-Pet off and push it back into my pocket. I might feed it after all.

Tom is already crossing the courtyard. I pick up the fallen lantern while the King retrieves the gun.

"I shall keep this musket." He decides. "It may yet be useful, although I confess I find it a coward's weapon."

It's dark and cold inside the prison. The stone walls are damp and I can hear the DRIP DRIP of water – a freezing drop runs down my neck and I almost shout. We use the lamp to find our way and climb down a flight of narrow steps that are so wet they're slippery.

"William?" Tom whispers in a loud voice as we reach the cells. Wooden doors in rows, all locked. It's the most miserable place I've ever been, and I include school in that.

"Tom?" Grandpa Bill's voice floats through one of the doors. Tom rattles the handle but it doesn't open.

"Where's the key?" He asks. But none of us have the key.

"Stand aside." The King aims the gun at the lock and shoots. The BANG is so loud it echoes around the stone walls about ten times before it fades away. The cell door swings open and Grandpa Bill peers out. I don't wait for him to speak, I just leap into his arms and hug him. For a wonderful moment I'm back in my own time and everything's normal again.

"Vicky? Why haven't you gone home?"

I look up into the face that always gave me Kitkats and pocket money. He looks old and tired and there's a big bruise over one eye.

"I don't know how to go home." I admit. "I've got the right coin, but I don't know how to make the Winds of Time do anything." I push my hand into my pocket and hunt for the coin. To my irritation, I can't find it. What I do find is a little hole in the pocket lining.

"I think I've lost it." I say crossly. "I'll have to get another."

Grandpa Bill stares at me.

"There is no other."

"What?"

"I only have *one* coin from 2020 Vicky. And that was only in case of emergencies. So you're stuck here until we find it."

My stomach sinks. I think of that long, dark, dirt track Tom and I rode on. The coin could be *anywhere.* It could be buried deep in the mud by now.

"We must leave now. Hurry." The King tosses the gun to the side, Grandpa Bill bows to him again.

"Sire, you shouldn't be here either. There's terrible danger. Poyntz's men have taken the City. You must leave."

"You are my friend William. I don't abandon my friends."

"I can't say I'm not grateful. Poyntz wants Thomas Carnsew. He suspects I know where he is."

"Do you?"

Grandpa Bill doesn't answer that, he just takes my hand and we retrace our steps back towards the courtyard.

We did it.

We broke into a prison and saved Grandpa Bill. Nobody will *ever* believe this. Not ever. Our feet echo against the stone as we head for the way out. Then I'm going to have to start hunting for that coin, unless I want to spend my life in a long dress with no Internet.

I wonder what time it is? The arched doorway ahead looks lighter than it did, so maybe the sun's rising. I check the watch. It says 3.20am. That's a bit early for sunrise, but it's probably wrong. I never set it once the hands started moving.

We emerge into the light.

Only it's not *sunlight*. It's *torchlight*.

There are about ten men on horses, all of them with guns, facing us. We stop. I recognise the guard we chased away with the Pocket-Pet.

General Poyntz looks at the King; his eyes are icy-cold. He doesn't bow. I wasn't expecting to see him. Why isn't he still asleep?

"Charles Stuart. I'm arresting you in the name of God and England." His voice rings out.

"You do nothing in the name of God." The King says without shouting. "For I have the divine right to rule. Your rebellion is a rebellion against God."

They both think God's on their side. I wonder if he is? Or maybe he's just letting them fight it out and not getting involved. The King's actually quite brave though, I'm sorry he's going to get his head chopped off quite soon.

I feel someone at my shoulder. Grandpa Bill presses a coin into my hand. I clutch it, not understanding.

"The words." He whispers into my ear. "Say the words."

"What words?" I whisper back. General Poyntz looks very pleased with himself. I hope Gertrude and Anne are okay. I wonder what happened to *he'll sleep until sunrise?*

"I also hear you are harbouring a witch." He looks directly at me and his smile is even more crocodile-like than Gertrude's.

"*Say the words.*" Grandpa's whisper is even more urgent. "Or do you want to be hanged? The words on the watch."

Then I understand. I take a quick breath and squeeze the coin.

"*Winds of Time take me away, to the day before today. Choose a coin to pay the fee and Father Time will honour thee.*" I mumble, my words tumbling over themselves like a waterfall. General Poyntz doesn't take his eyes off me.

"Are you casting a spell, witch? Or are you summoning up demons?"

"She has a demon in a magic egg General." The guard I frightened earlier comes to his side. He has a fat, squashy face and lots of fuzzy hair. General Poyntz is thinner, his face looks hard. Like he has trouble smiling.

"Does she indeed? I'm certain she'll confess everything. Given the opportunity."

The tone of his voice is scarier than Mr. Hodgeman's when I've forgotten to do my homework. Which is quite a lot. I swallow, the coin feels hot in my hand. A breeze blows past my ear. I tighten my fingers.

"I'm sorry I called you dumb." I whisper. "You're not dumb. Just get me out of here. Please."

I screw up my eyes just as the wind hits. A warm, strong wind that pushes me backwards. I don't fight it, not this time. This time I'll let it take me wherever it wants to go.

Chapter Eight

Some Random Girl

I don't trust the Winds of Time.

Wind isn't supposed to deliberately scoop you up and take you away. It's supposed to dry the washing on the line and maybe blow your irritating brother's Lego figures off his windowsill. That's all. It isn't supposed to get involved in your life, taking you from time to time like a train.

I have no idea where the wind's taking me, but I feel its strength as it lifts me from my feet. I don't want to be hanged as a witch, but I don't want to leave Grandpa Bill and Tom and the King behind because I didn't like the way General Poyntz stared at them. Like he was a hungry owl and they were tasty looking field-mice.

I open an eye.

It's not dark any more. The sun and the moon move overhead like Grandpa Bill's watch, going east to west in seconds. It makes me feel dizzy, watching them.

I land with a bump again and lie still for a moment, staring up into the sky.

"Are you okay love?"

A fat woman with a blue summer dress and matching handbag helps me sit up. "Wherever did you come from?" The woman looks normal, like she belongs in my time. The proper time.

I glance around. I'm still at Chester Castle, only there are modern cars, and women in jeans, and a sign pointing to Chester's tourist attractions.

I'm back.

Was I ever away? Did I dream it? Maybe I came to Chester for a day out and fell and hit my head.

Something burns my hand and I drop the coin. It lands by my feet and disappears with a hiss and a sizzle.

"It it fancy dress love?" The woman asks, noting my long skirts. "Are you with him?"

I turn.

Then I almost fall over in surprise. Or in horror.

The King. The *actual* King of England from 1645, is sitting in the courtyard beside me, looking really bemused.

"Yes." I say, scrambling to my feet. "We're tour guides. We dress up as different historical characters."

By now a small crowd has gathered.

"Oh right," Someone says. "He's meant to be King Charles right? It's a very good costume. Can I have a photo?"

Inside I'm screaming. How on *earth* did I bring the King back home with me? What are the stupid Winds of Time playing at?

"You look a bit young to be tour guide." The woman squints at me.

"It's just for fun." I assure her, and I help the King to his feet. I need to get him away.

"Don't say anything." I hiss in his ear. "Not a word. Just walk."

Still confused, he does so, until we reach the road and he sees the cars.

The he gives a yell and everybody turns and stares at us.

"What demons are those!" He cries, backing away. I hold his arm tightly.

"Just cars." I assure him. "Like metal horses. Sort of. They won't hurt you."

"But that terrible roaring?"

"It's just their engines. Come on."

We're not too far from the river where we left out horses three-hundred and fifty years ago. They'll be long dead now.

So will Tom.

And Gertrude.

And Anne.

We reach a quiet bench overlooking the river and we sit down together.

"What happened?" I ask him. "This is 2020. You don't belong here."

He still looks really puzzled.

"William gave me a coin." He opens his hand. He has a little burn mark on his palm which means he didn't drop it quickly enough.

"But Grandpa didn't have any more coins from 2020." I say. "He certainly didn't have two of them."

"2020?"

I think about how Gertrude and the others spoke. "The year of our Lord Two thousand and twenty." I tell him. There's a bin on the other side of the bench with a newspaper poking out of it, flapping in the breeze. I pull it out and show him the front page. "See."

"Nineteen hundred and ninety-nine." The King reads. I turn the paper and stare down at the words.

1999.

Seriously? I'm not home after all. I'm still twenty years in the past.

My heart sinks. That means I can't go home. Mum and Dad don't even meet until 2002. Mum still lives with Grandpa Bill and Uncle Tommy.

My thoughts trail off. Grandpa Bill and Uncle Tommy live just outside Chester, in Rowton. It's the same house Mum and I were clearing out. But I can't just turn up saying *hi, I'm your granddaughter from the future, this is the King of*

England from 1645. Can you help us?

But Grandpa Bill, the one from this time, might at least be able to give us some coins from 1645 so we can go back, and then I can find the only coin from 2020 that exists before 2020. Who knows, maybe Grandpa Bill was already travelling in time in the 1990s. Maybe he's been doing it all his life.

I sit back on the bench and watch a seagull peck half a sandwich. The King watches a car go past, and then a girl in a short skirt. Then I remember how confused I felt when I first turned up in 1645.

"I know it's weird." I say kindly. "This is the future. It's still my past. I won't be born for another ten years." I watch an aeroplane cut through the clouds far above my head. "But it's *almost* right."

Bet there's still no decent Internet though.

"I should have faced Poyntz. Not run away like a frightened woman."

I face him. "Right. First of all. Stop saying women are weak. Or scared. Or should do what they're told. That stuff hasn't been acceptable since the 1960s. Secondly. Poyntz is dead. He'll have been dead for three hundred years."

"But I have a battle to fight for my throne. My right as King. I must show Parliament that they oppose God Himself when they oppose me."

A man walks past with a dog and looks at us oddly. The King's costume is pretty eye-catching.

He needs to find something normal to wear, if he's going to blend in.

We don't have any money, so we have to walk right across the city. Two tourists stop and ask us for photographs. I'm glad to find nobody knows what a *selfie* is in 1999 otherwise everyone would end up with a picture of the King of England on their phones. But the only mobiles I see being used are big, clunky things with no cameras or Internet access.

"Grandpa Bill – that is, William Tremayne - might not know you yet." I warn him as we cross the road. He watches the little green man flash with the fascination of a toddler gazing at Christmas lights. And he stares into the window of every shop we go past, distracted by everything from fashions to fluffy toys.

"Truly, this future is a hideous place." He says more than once. I feel totally insulted. I thought the past was pretty hideous.

"At least I don't need to ride a horse and I can get rid of this stupid dress."

"Do all the maids go around with so few clothes?"

"We just wear what we like. Women have equality now."

I don't know whether he really understands. But maybe it's harder to adapt to the future than the past. At least I know a bit about the past. I even have family there. I mean, if Gertrude Carnsew is Grandpa Bill's great-grandmother nine times removed she must be my great-grandmother eleven times removed. And if Tom is her son he must be my great-grandfather ten times removed.

I think about this. That rude little boy is my ancestor. I don't know how I feel about that. It's strange to think he's been dead for so long and yet I only saw him a couple of hours ago.

Grandpa Bill's house is just like I remember it before it got really old and shabby. It's a big, four-bedroom detached house near the canal with an iron fence and a garden full of stocks and foxgloves with a birdbath and a bronze knocker on the door shaped like a lion.

It's like stepping back into an old family photograph. I remember Jonathan used to chase me around and around the birdbath until I was dizzy, and I used to look for fairy rings on the lawn. I still do sometimes.

I knock on the door and wait. After a few moments I hear footsteps and then the door swings open.

A younger version of my mother smiles at me from the doorway. She's about twenty, and very pretty, with a book in her hand, her thumb marking the page she's reading. It's weird though, like someone's put a filter over her and washed out all her wrinkles. She's wearing headphones and pulls them away from her ears so she can talk to us.

"Hi?" She looks at us both blankly and pops her gum. We must look pretty odd in these ancient clothes. "Can I help?"

"Um. Is Grandpa – I mean – is Bill Tremayne home?"

"That's my Dad. He and uncle Tommy are in the back garden. I'll take you through." The King takes off his hat and bows, which makes her laugh.

We follow her into the hallway. It's exactly like I remember with the diamond-shaped floor-tiles and the tall grasses in a big terracotta vase. I forgot how nice it used to look before all the books and the newspapers took over. I know the way through to the back garden but we follow mum politely. I feel so strange. I just want to hug her, but she's not mum yet. Not the mum I know anyway.

Mum opens the big patio doors and we step out into the sunshine and onto the paving slabs with all the little blue flowers that creep between the cracks. A much younger Grandpa Bill is mowing the grass and Uncle Tommy is dead-heading the yellow rose with a pair of secateurs.

"Dad. Visitors." She yells.

"Thank you my lady." The King bows again and again she gives a funny giggle. Then she heads off over the garden to carry on reading. She always loved the stone seat by the lilies. That's her name.

Lilly. It feels funny to see a moment of the life that now only exists in the stories she tells.

"I do think that lady to be quite beautiful." The King says in my ear. I frown.

"That's my mum. I mean. She will be my mum." I look him in the eye. He has quite nice, expressive eyes. "So she's going to marry my Dad." In about four years. There's definitely a Timewalkers episode where they go back in time and someone marries the wrong person and then the hero isn't born at all. He'd better not get any ideas. Nobody's going to stop me being born.

I'm not so bothered about Jonathan being born though.

Grandpa Bill and Uncle Tommy stop their work and look at us. Then they look at each other, then back at us with expressions exactly like a dead fish. It must run in the family. They both drop what they're doing and run towards us like they're being chased by a dragon.

They reach the patio and stare as if we've just grown two heads each. I wish they recognised me. I don't like being a stranger. I felt more at home at Carnsew Hall. At least Gertrude knew I was family. Here, I'm just some random girl.

Then Uncle Tommy bows. Just like he believes the King to actually be the King, and not some guy dressed up.

"Hello Thomas Carnsew." The King says. "So this is where you've been hiding."

Chapter Nine

A Rum Do

Uncle Tommy makes coffee and juice and brings it to the summerhouse by the pond at the bottom of the garden. I don't feel as much at home as I thought I would. It's just all a little bit wrong. Wrong ages. Wrong time.

I can't believe my Uncle Tommy is Thomas Carnsew though. Tom's Dad. I mean, how does that work?

"Poyntz wanted me dead sire." Uncle Tommy sips his coffee and the light hits his bald head the way it always does. "William Tremayne brought me here for my safety."

"Whilst you leave your wife and son behind? That is the action of a coward sir."

"It was my intention to return soon. When Poyntz has forgotten me."

"Sydnam Poyntz will not forget you. He will continue to make Gertrude Carsew's life a misery while he hunts you."

"In 1650 he will leave England and travel to the West Indies. I will return then."

But he never does. He never goes back because he's an old man in 2020. He was at Grandpa Bill's funeral. That means Tom and Gertrude never know what happens to him. That means he hides in the future for the rest of his life.

"I don't get any of this." I say, picking at a piece of cherry cake. "It's all mixed up."

Uncle Tommy laughs. "I have never understood the Winds of Time. Only Chronos himself comprehends."

"Chronos?"

He nods. "Time."

"You mean *Father Time*?" The rhyme that activates the coins mentions Father Time. Or maybe the coins activate the rhyme. I don't quite know.

Grandpa Bill joins us. He looks so much younger it's like he's a different person. He gazes at me and I gaze back.

"You look so much like Lilly." He says at last.

"She's my mum."

He sits and surveys this odd gathering of people caught out of time.

"Well now, this is a rum do isn't it?"

A *rum do?* That's one of Grandpa Bill's expressions. It's what he says when Jonathan tries to show him how to buy stuff online for the millionth time.

I think, sitting around a table with two people born about four-hundred years ago and one who won't be born for another ten years is a bit more than a *rum do.*

"What's going on Grandpa?" I ask, because I really need to understand. I also need a Mars Bar, a good night's sleep and to binge-watch Timewalkers. "When did you start all this time-travel stuff?"

He doesn't answer at once, just stirs some sugar into his coffee.

"You could say it's in our blood Vicky. Our family tree."

"I found our family tree. Well, some of it. It goes right back to William the Conqueror."

He nods. "It does. Yes. How does it feel to have the blood of Kings running through your veins?"

I shrug. "It doesn't really matter, does it?" It's not like I'm going to end up on the throne.

"Oh, it matters. But not the way you think. Though I admit it took me a long time to understand."

He nods at my wrist. And I realise we're both wearing the same watch, twenty years apart. He taps his.

"No matter how hard you try, you can't outrun time. You can't escape what you are."

"What I am?"

"The Winds of Time don't blow for just *anyone* Vicky. Otherwise people would be jumping from time to time like grasshoppers. And that would never do. No, Father Time has to keep it all running smoothly see. Time."

"This isn't making any sense Grandpa." Has he been drinking? Like that Christmas mum still doesn't like to mention.

"Father Time holds back the Winds of Time."

"Right. But *Father Time* is just an expression. Like *Mother Nature* or *Jack Frost*. He's not a real person."

Grandpa Bill looks at me the way he looked at me when I thought tadpoles were raisins with long tails. That was Jonathan's fault okay? He told me that.

And he told me marshmallows were bits of snow preserved in a jar with sugar. For three winters I tried to make them but mine just kept melting. I was *five!*

"Of *course* Father Time is a real person Vicky." He tells me. "Who do you think keeps the Winds of Time in check? The tooth fairy?" He laughs at his own joke. I don't.

Grandpa Bill roots around in his pocket, then drops a handful of odds and ends onto the table in front of us. Two modern coins, an elastic band, a safety pin, a sweet in a plastic wrapper and a really ancient coin so battered there are no markings left on it.

"Let me show you." He says. Then he taps the table twice.

"Winds of Time, blow true and fast,

Beyond the now and to the past."

I don't get a chance to point out those are the wrong words before a blast of wind hits the whole garden so hard its like a hurricane. I think I squeal as the trees bend around us and the flowers flatten and I have to cling onto my chair to stop myself crashing backwards. Over by the stone seat, mum's book flies away, and out of the corner of my eye I see the King run to catch it before it can disappear up into the sky. His long hair and hat flap madly around his ears and he holds them on his head.

The things from Grandpa's pocket are all scooped up in the wind. I watch them swirl above my head, dancing together, joined by flower petals and twigs, before they vanish completely. The coffee-cups and plates roll off the table and smash on the stone floor.

Grandpa Bill and Uncle Tommy don't move at all.

The wind drops sharply and everything looks normal again, except a few of the foxgloves have lost their flowers and somewhere at the other side of the garden I can hear mum complaining about the *rotten weather* to somebody.

I blink and push my hair out of my face.

Then I look at table and I give a little squeak of surprise.

The objects Grandpa put there haven't moved at all.

Which is impossible. I saw them fly away.

But they haven't moved.

What they have done, however, is *change.*

I lean forwards and pick up one of the coins. A moment ago it was a shiny gold pound. Now it looks ancient. I turn it over in my fingers, most of the markings have been rubbed away. What happened to it?

The second coin is in an even worse state. It looks like something from a museum. The safety-pin is bent and orange with rust. There's nothing but a slightly dark line of what could be dust left where the elastic band was. There's still something left of the plastic wrapper, though not of the sweet that was inside. It's just sort of black-green mouldy stuff.

"Plastic takes a very long time to rot away." Grandpa Bill remarks, sipping his coffee. The only cup that didn't overturn and roll away in the wind. "People need to remember that. It's not good for the environment. But they you go. That's a thousand years. What do you think?"

I try to touch what was once the elastic band but it crumbles to nothing. "A thousand years?"

"The Winds of Time took all these things away for a thousand years. It's always the same location mind. Remember that. Time can't take anyone to see the pyramids being built like Tommy here wanted. To do that you'd need to get to Egypt the old fashioned way and then ask the Winds of Time to take you back. Though they like their coins. You could probably use a bit of gold or jewellery from the right era though."

I try to pick up the other coin, The one that already looked ancient, but it gives a little sizzle and disappears. Just like the coin that took me to 1645 and the one that brought me here.

"That was from 1064. Even before William the Conqueror took the throne. They're not easy to get hold of so don't make me waste another."

"So these things? They all went back in time? Like I did?"

"That's how it works. But the Winds need a bit of help. Something to lock onto. Coins are best because they have exact years on them. Anything old will work though, so you need to be careful.

And always carry this year's coin in your pocket, just in case."

"But I didn't come back from 1645 all wrinkly and ancient."

"Of course not. But you only stayed for a few hours. These are just *things*. They can't say the rhyme and get back like you can. So they stayed the full thousand years. They only just caught up with us."

He picks up the faded coins and puts them back in his pocket. "The Winds of Time blow in more than one direction Vicky. Father Time has to keep them blowing from present to future."

"But Father Time isn't *real!*" He's not a *person.* It's just – well – I don't know what it is really. It's just *there*. Like the air or the water.

"Father Time makes the flowers grow. He gives us sunny springs and snowy winters. Harvests and Easter and Christmas in the right order. He makes babies into children and gives old people a million memories. How much more real do you want?"

I give a massive yawn. I feel like I've been awake for days and days. Uncle Tommy gathers up the broken china from the cups and I rest my head in my hands, I don't think I can make sense of any of this right now. Father Time and the Civil War and coins and magic rhymes. It's all so ridiculous.

"And Father Time makes sure you go to sleep one day and wake up safely the next." I hear Grandpa Bill say just before I fall fast asleep.

Chapter Ten

Because History

Now I really am dreaming.

I know I'm dreaming because I'm

lying on a bed in the spare room at Grandpa Bill's

house, back when it wasn't full of junk and dust,

and I'm staring at the picture of Old Father Time

on the wall. I'm looking at his thin, scraggy

muscles and the way his eyebrows are low over his

mean, hungry eyes.

I *hated* that painting as a child and I hate it now.

It shouldn't be in this room. There should be a nice

picture of a bridge over a pond full of water-lilies in this room.

I turn over in bed. It feels like the old man's eyes are burning into me. I don't want to look at him. I don't.

My eyes snap open and I sit up. It's dark outside, Grandpa Bill's watch says 2.20am and a thin strip of moonlight hits the painting making it really look as if Old Father Time's eyes are glinting.

Climbing out of bed I take hold of the picture, intending to turn it to face the wall so it can't look at me any more.

Then I stop.

I stop and I stare.

The hourglass in the man's skinny hand is moving. Or seems to be. I look closer. I can *see* the sand running out into the bottom of the glass. I can even *hear* the soft swoosh.

Spooked, I glance up into the man's painted face. It's an old picture, it must be since the big version is hanging at Carnsew Hall in 1645. I wonder just how old it is?

The eyes blink.

This time I yell and fall backwards, pulling the bedclothes off on top of me. He actually *blinked*. Those pale grey eyes are looking back at me.

"Are you okay?"

Mum rushes into the room just like she always does when I have a bad dream. She's wearing a nightie with two elephants on the front and still has a book in her hand – a different one this time.

I sit, tangled in the bedclothes, staring up at the picture.

"It – moved. It's eyes -"

Mum kneels beside me and helps untwist the sheet from my leg. She *feels* like mum. Suddenly I want my real mum so much it hurts and I burst into tears.

"Hey – don't cry. It's okay." She puts her arms around me. "It's just a creepy old painting. It freaks me out sometimes too. I don't know why Dad won't just chuck it in the bin. It's the first thing I'll do, if I ever inherit this place."

She helps me back to bed and sits beside me. "Things always look scary in the dark. That's why I like to read at night. Then I can be somewhere else."

I turn my back and pull the bedclothes over my head. Mum pats my shoulder.

"I like your friend."

"My friend?" My friends won't be born for ten years. Even then they won't be much fun until they're out of nappies.

"Charles."

I sit up again.

"He's very charming. He saved my book from blowing away in the wind. Then he kissed my hand."

Warning bells go off in my head. No *way* is mum allowed to fall in love with the King. He's going back to get the chop just as soon as possible.

"It must be so much fun, dressing up and guiding tourists around those big houses. I was thinking of applying for a job at Sydnam Hall. I'd get to dress up as a maid."

I lie back down in bed.

It'll be fine I tell myself. The King'll be gone by tomorrow then mum'll meet Dad and everything'll be all right.

Mum stands up. "Night night. Sleep tight. Don't let the bugs bite."

I finish the rhyme automatically.

"If they do. Get a shoe. And split their little heads in two."

She laughs. "That's so strange. I thought that was just something Dad said to me."

"I bet you'll say it to your kids. When you have some." I snuggle down. I refuse to look at that stupid old painting again. The last thing I hear before falling asleep again is the door clicking shut.

Next morning the sun washes away any of the fears of last night and mum finds a whole box of clothes from when she was a kid at the bottom of the wardrobe. "Dad's such a hoarder." She laughs, pulling out some pretty old-fashioned jeans. "He'll still have my baby stuff somewhere too."

I find some suitable clothes and run downstairs to the familiar-smelling kitchen with the yellow curtains and the herbs growing on the windowsill. The herb-box is still there in my time but there were only brown sticks and a dandelion the last time I checked. I suppose being away in 1645 makes it hard to water your plants.

Grandpa Bill is making breakfast, bacon sizzles in the pan and there are cornflakes already on the table. I take a bowl and sit down.

"Where's the King?"

"Poking through my books. You shouldn't have brought him here. We don't want time to get too messy."

I pour milk from the milk-bottle. "I didn't send him. *You* did. The other you. From the future. In the past." I think time is already pretty messy. "And anyway, you brought Uncle Tommy through."

"As a favour."

"We can send him back can't we? The King."

"Only if we can find another coin from 1645."

I look up from my breakfast. I'd assumed Grandpa Bill had plenty of the right coins.

"They don't grow on trees you know. Tommy brought plenty with him, but we've used them up now. Civil War coins are collector's items. Now Victorian pennies? I've got hundreds of those."

He brings a cup of coffee to the table. "There's a collector's fair today. I'm hoping I can pick up the odd one. They won't come cheap though."

I finish my cereal. "Why doesn't Uncle Tommy go back? I mean, he can just go straight back to 1650. Why's he hanging round here?"

Grandpa Bill sits beside me, our matching watches almost touch.

"Vicky. Uncle Tommy can't go back. Not ever."

"Why? Gertrude and Tom love him. They really miss him."

"And I miss them." I turn around, Uncle Tommy is in the doorway. I find it hard to imagine him in those long boots and with the sort of big hat the King wears. He always looks *sort* of old-fashioned, but old-fashioned *vintage,* shirts and waistcoats, not old-fashioned three centuries ago. "I miss them so much my heart aches."

"So go and see them."

"I cannot."

"Why?" I push. I want to know.

He stares at me, then looks away. "Because I *died* Vicky. I died in the battle of Rowton Heath on the 24th September 1645. I left my wife and son to fight for the King and I never returned."

"But I *saw* that battle. You weren't there." Or maybe he was. It's not like I saw everyone.

"Not this time, no."

"But it only happened *once.*" I look at Grandpa Bill, trying to understand. "Isn't that really messing with time?"

"Of course it's messing with time." Grandpa snaps, standing sharply and throwing his coffee-cup into the sink. "But why should he have wasted his life dying in a pointless battle?"

"Because *history.* That's why." I can't believe Grandpa Bill would change time like that. If this was an episode of Timewalkers something awful would have happened to the future by now.

I feel cold in the pit of my stomach.

Maybe something awful *has* happened to the future.

"There's history and there's family Vicky. I made a judgement call and chose family. So sue me."

He's not even sorry. He took a man out of one century and dropped him in another and he isn't even sorry.

"Do you do that a lot? Steal people out of history?" I stand up. I feel very grown-up suddenly.

"Only my family. To keep them safe."

"And why is our family so important? People *die*. You can't stop them dying just because they're family."

He gives me a funny look, like I'm too young to understand.

"I can and I will." He says in a flat, cold voice. Then scoops up his car-keys from a bowl on the counter. The warm sun feels cold on my arms. None of the good guys in Timewalkers ever said anything like that. They just all make speeches about how you can't change time no matter what happens.

Well, I won't change time.

"Stay here. I'll be back soon. I need to find those coins." And then he leaves. Just like that. Without even saying goodbye.

I leave my bowl in the sink and head through to the sitting room. Grandpa's bookshelves are full the way they always are. He still bought books, even when Jonathan taught him how to use the Internet.

In fact, the only thing he used the Internet for was to buy more books. There are fresh flowers on the piano and the big, French windows face the garden.

The King stands in the corner of the room, nose buried in a book. He hasn't put any ordinary clothes on yet so he still looks like he's in costume.

"We'll get you back today." I tell him, hopeful Uncle Bill will be able to track down the right coin. "We could go to Sydnam hall. That'd be safest." I've thought about that a lot. General Poyntz saw us disappear. He'll have no idea where we'll arrive back or even if we'll arrive back. And I want to see Gertrude and Anne before I start combing the area for that 2020 coin.

The King barely nods. Then he lifts his head from the book and gazes at me as if he's just watched his puppy-dog run over. Too late I realise the book in his hands is *The Complete History of the Stuart Monarchs.*

Oops.

"I die." He says in a quiet, puzzled voice. "I'm executed by my own people. In four years time." And he looks so sad I want to give him a cuddle.

Chapter Eleven

It Was Grandpa Bill All Along

"I am King by the grace of God. How can I be executed? What crime did I commit?"

Seriously? He wants an answer? He expects an eleven year-old kid who doesn't even know when World War Two ended to explain why a seventeenth century King got his head lopped off?

I shrug. "You shouldn't read any more."

But I think he might already have read too much.

"My death brings a period of misery to this country. There will be no sport. No theatre. No Christmas. All the simple pleasures, stripped from my people." He's angry, and I realise he's not just scared to die, but he actually cares about the country too.

"And you?" He looks up from the page. "And William Tremayne? You knew and said nothing?"

"Hey, I'm just a girl. Like you'd have listened to anything *I* said."

"God's wounds!" He hurls the book across the room and it smashes into a glass cabinet full of china figurines. That's weird because there was never a cabinet there anyway. But that can't be because someone I brought back from the past smashed it.

"I will not let them do it! I will not kneel to the likes of Cromwell and Poyntz. I will fight them all."

He draws his sword and I leap back as he stabs a cushion in sheer fury, slashing through the fabric.

"God Himself will fight on my side. He will smite the arrogance of the Roundheads from the face of the earth."

He swings around, slicing his sword through the curtain and stopping about five centimetres from Mum's neck.

Mum doesn't move, caught half in, half out of the French windows. She doesn't drop her book though, nor does she take her eyes from the sharp blade until he moves it away.

"Apologies my Lady." The King recovers and sheaths his sword. Then he bows to Mum. "I received some distressing news."

Mum looks at the broken cabinet and the slashed cushion.

"I'm sorry. Can I help?"

The King takes her hand and kisses it gallantly. "Indeed you can. Take me away from here. Take me to a place where I can drown my sorrows in a flagon of ale."

Ale? That's like beer or something isn't it?

That might not be a good idea.

Mum grins. "It's a bit early for the pubs to be open. But it's a lovely day. Why don't I show you the city."

"No." I yell. Is she stupid? "He has to wait here. He might change history."

Mum doesn't seem impressed. "What?"

"I mean – wearing those funny clothes – he can't go out."

Mum laughs and tosses her hair off her shoulders and gives the King a smile I've only ever seen her give Dad. "I think he looks fabulous." *Fabulous?* She's changed her tune. She told Jonathan he looked ridiculous when he insisted on dressing like Luke Sykwalker for a whole year.

"Come on." Mum pulls him towards the door. "Let me show you King Charles' Tower. It's supposed to be where Charles the First watched his army lose in 1645."

That's about as sensitive as when Jonathan broke his ankle and mum told him to *hop it.* I groan, but the King doesn't seem to mind. I hear their footsteps in the hallway and the front door slam behind them.

I flop down on the sofa and hardly notice all the white stuffing that's still falling out of the cushion. Mum's finally left her book behind. I pick it up.

I'm amazed to realise it's one of the original Timewalkers novels from the 1970s, back before the TV series got rebooted with a massive budget. The picture is a grainy photo of the characters. I've never tried watching the original series because the sets all look rubbish. But maybe I should. Then mum and I could talk about it together.

I lie flat on the sofa and watch a spider crawl across the ceiling. Lucky old spider. It doesn't have any weird stuff to worry about. All it needs to do is spin webs and eat flies. Suddenly I long for my old, boring life. I want to annoy Jonathan and watch TV and eat chocolate digestives and play Animal-Crossy.

I doze a little, half dreaming. Still hoping I'll wake up and find myself in my own bed. But I think I've finally accepted all this is real. I hope Grandpa Bill finds the coins we need and I can dump the King back where he belongs and go back home. After this I'm never, *ever* going to touch cash again. I don't trust coins any more.

Something jolts me awake, some crash from upstairs and I roll off the sofa and onto the carpet where I scramble to my feet. It sounded like it came from my room.

I run up the stairs and peer into the spare bedroom and the rumpled bed. I've never seen the point in making a bed; I'm only going to mess it up again.

The horrible portrait of Father Time has fallen off the wall and is now lying, face down, on the floor. That was the crash I heard. Well, I don't much care if that particular picture is ruined. The window hangs open, still moving in the wind. I slam it shut, then pick up the painting and drag it back to its hook, trying not to look into those cruel eyes but failing. That's what I feel he is. Cruel.

Once on the wall I stare at the twisted features of the old man. I don't mean to look, but once I've met those eyes again I can't look away.

I don't like him. Whatever he's thinking, they're not nice thoughts.

"What *are* you thinking?" I ask the painting, rubbing at a scratch on the wooden frame.

My eyes are drawn to the hourglass again. That's odd, before the sands had almost run down to the bottom. Now they're in the top, just like it's been turned over.

I study his face again and I almost scream.

The old man's face has changed. Now I know him. He looks older. Harder. I might not even have recognised him had I not seen that same hardness in his eyes today.

The man in the portrait, bent, cloaked and carrying a scythe, is Grandpa Bill.

I back away. This is *impossible*. It's changed, but so subtly I'm starting to think it was Grandpa Bill all along. Perhaps it was. I think about the painting that scared me as a child and I realise that's why it scared me, because it looked like a really nasty version of Grandpa Bill.

But Grandpa Bill is *nice*. He's nothing like this horrible creature all hunched up and clutching his hourglass like some monster out of Greek Mythology.

I run, rattling down the stairs, through the front door and out into the clean sunshine.

It's my imagination. That's all. A walk will clear my head and when I get back Grandpa Bill might have found the coin.

Then I remember. There's an antique shop about a mile away. Or, at least, there is in my time, but I think it's been there for decades. Perhaps they'll have a 1645 coin. It's worth a try anyway. Not that I have any money, but I could go and look.

Feeling a lot more cheerful I let my feet find their way along the familiar roads, past familiar gardens and not-so familiar gardens until I reach the little row of shops. They've changed a bit, but *David Green and son Antiques,* is still where it always was. Or will be. There's even that same suit of armour in the window. I doubt anyone wants to buy a suit of armour. Unless they have a way of going back in time.

The shop window is full of old pots, jewellery, figurines, vases and ancient books. I stare through the glass at a tray of coins, but most of them seem to be no more than a hundred years old.

I squint and focus on the shop interior. It's packed full of all sorts of old paintings and big sculptures, there's even a stuffed animal or two. It's not very busy either, I can only see two customers in the shop.

Then the woman turns around and I realise it's mum. I really, *really* hope the King's still with her.

I can't possibly let a man who thinks he has a God-given right to rule England but doesn't know how electricity works wander around on his own. He won't sound sane.

I push open the heavy door and the bell rings above my head. The King's still with her at least. That's something.

"I say you are a thief sir!" He's shouting at the little fat man behind the counter. "This is my Bible, inscribed here to me by my own wife. Give it back at once."

He's suddenly very loud and seems to fill the shop, Mum backs away, I don't think she likes him as much any more. Good. She sees me and hurries over.

"He's quite mad." She whispers. "He saw a Bible in the window and swears it belongs to him."

It probably does.

The King draws his sword, but there's not a lot of room in the shop and he knocks a stuffed rabbit onto the floor with his elbow.

"Give me what is mine sir, or by Heaven, I shall take it."

He seems a bit – I don't know – more *shouty* than before. More like Grandpa Bill was that Christmas mum doesn't talk about. When he got drunk.

"Has he had something to drink?" I ask. Mum shrugs.

"We bought a few cans from the off-licence." She says helplessly, showing me a plastic carrier-bag that's probably going still going to be polluting the planet in a thousand years time. "He's only had two."

I'm going to make a guess she doesn't mean cans of Coke. Great. The soon-to-be beheaded time-displaced King of England, with a sword, a bit drunk in an antique shop. Could my life get any worse?

Don't answer that. Of course it could.

The King swings his sword, the owner ducks

and it slices straight through what I think was a

tapestry. Well, now it's *two* tapestries.

"I insist you put that away." The owner covers

his head with his arms. "I've had that Bible for at

least twenty years and – and if you don't go right

now I'll call the police. I will."

The King doesn't take any notice and instead

spins around and attacks the suit of armour, his

sword clashing against the metal with a horrible

CLANG.

"How dare you withhold what is mine, Have at

thee." And he starts to lunge at the armour as

though it's fighting back. Books, china, jugs,

ornaments of all description are knocked from the shelves and the armour sways as if it's drunk too. I have to get him out of here before he -

CRASH

Too late. The suit of armour smashes to the floor. Bits of it fly in all directions. One of the gauntlets hits me right on the shoulder. I didn't realise armour was so heavy.

"Yield sir, to your King."

I grab the King's arm.

"He's yielded see? Totally yielded. Yay you. You won. Congratulations." I shove and pull him out of the musty old shop and into the street.

"But my Bible. The rogue has stolen it."

I can hear mum trying to smooth things over with the owner. I hope she doesn't end up with a huge bill for damages. For a moment I'm glad she doesn't know who I am or I could probably kiss Kirkbury ComicCon goodbye until I'm about sixteen.

"We can go back and buy your Bible later." I promise. If we're not banned from the stupid shop forever.

"And stay out!" The owner shouts after us; he sounds a whole lot braver now there's no sword at his throat.

With any luck though, I'll stay out until at least 2020.

Chapter Twelve

Which Means I'll Be Born

Somehow mum and I manhandle

the King back towards Grandpa

Bill's house.

"You can't just walk into shops and take stuff."

I tell him, as we drop down to the canal towpath.

At least it's quiet here, there are fewer people to stare at his out-of-place clothing.

"Can I not?" I wish he wouldn't shout. The long hair, puffy-sleeved jacket-thing and frilly collar are enough to attract attention without him bellowing at the top of his voice.

And the sword. He keeps drawing it and swinging it round. That thing's *sharp.*

"I am King of England. I can do whatever I wish, for mine is a divine right that no man may take from me."

"Does he really think he's King Charles the first?" Mum whispers, only she doesn't whisper quietly enough.

"My Lady, I am indeed King Charles, and I am glad to learn my son with succeed me when Cromwell's treacherous rule is at an end." I *really* wish I hadn't let him read that book. Now he knows more about his future than I do.

He lunges at a duck with his sword, misses, and it waddles away, looking quite upset at being bothered. I'm glad it's not far. I hope Grandpa Bill's back and I hope he managed to find the right coin.

The King stops so suddenly I almost fall over.

"I have come to a decision." He announces, bothering another family of ducks. "For the good of the country."

He stands on the towpath as if he's about to make a royal proclamation.

"I shall not return."

"What?"

"To my time."

I hope I heard that wrong.

"You can't *not* go back. You're part of history."

"As is Thomas Carnsew. No. I shall remain here where I shall not lose my head." He turns to me, eyes brighter than they were but weirdly bright, like he's a bit mad. "You girl, inform your King or Queen that I shall take the throne here, in this time."

"I can't just inform the Queen. She's the *Queen*. She's old and everyone likes her, even my Dad, and he doesn't think we should even *have* Kings and Queens because they cost too much."

He waves me away like I don't matter.

"I was chosen by God to rule, and by heaven, rule I shall."

I stamp my foot. "You have to go back. And you will. Just as soon as Grandpa Bill finds the right coin,"

The King sheaths his sword, then reaches into his jacket-thing. I think he calls it a *doublet,* whatever that is.

"Then you require money?"

He holds out a handful of coins. Even from here I can see at least one of them is dated 1645.

I stare at them.

"You had the right sort of coins all along? Why didn't you tell us?"

"You didn't ask." He says, closing his fingers over the precious coins. "However, if these coins can indeed transport me through time, I must be rid of them."

Then he **chucks** the whole handful into the canal. I watch them sink into the muddy water.

No. No. No. No.

I follow them.

Splash

It's not very deep. I know that because, in my time, Jonathan fell in once when he was feeding the ducks.

Okay. I *might* have pushed him. Just a little bit. In my defence he was saying he'd rather have a duck as a sister than me.

But I remember he could stand up in the water. So he didn't drown or anything. Which is why I always thought I shouldn't have got into *quite* as much trouble as I did. And it was really funny afterwards, when he had to squelch all the way home in wet clothes.

So I land in the canal, and I'm right, it's not very deep. On the bank mum watches with a horrified expression on her face.

"Just – don't let him go anyway." I say. Then I remember that she's a Timewalker fan too. "We can't mess up the fabric of time."

For a minute she looks totally confused. A little line forms between her eyebrows and she looks a bit more like the mum I know. Then she nods. I think mum's starting to realise this is real.

I look down into the water and try to reach the bottom with my hands. Only it's a bit too deep. I'm going to have to put my head underwater. Great.

Taking a deep breath I dive down into the cold, dirty water. *Please* don't let me swallow a big mouthful and end up with a tummy-bug for days.

Like Jonathan did.

It wasn't my fault. I didn't know swallowing filthy canal-water could land you in hospital. I felt awful afterwards and Jonathan knew I felt awful so he forgave me and shared his get-well-soon chocolate with me.

I miss my brother.

I never thought I'd think that, but I do.

I scrabble around in the mud and stones and bits of old tin cans and bike parts that litter the canal-bed, searching for something that feels like a coin. I find quite a few of them before I have to come up for air. Then I duck down and find more.

When I emerge from the canal, soggy and shivering, I have a handful of Civil-War coins. Some of them are real gold I think. They were heavy enough to sink straight to the bottom. I search my muddy palm and I'm delighted to find four of them are dated 1645. The others are a bit older so I shove them in my pocket.

On the bank, the King is down on one knee in front of mum. He's got another tin of whatever alcohol mum bought him and he's having trouble balancing.

"Marry me, sweet Lilly, and I shall make you Queen of England, Ireland and Scotland." He's saying, only he's slurring his words really badly so it sounds more like *Shcotland*. Mum looks embarrassed, like when Jonathan had a wee in the shrub section of the garden centre that time.

I grab his hand, pull the can out of it and give him one of the coins.

But he won't hold it.

So I pick it up and drop it down the top of his boot. He almost kicks me.

"Curses. I know your tricks. I shall not go back." He tries to put his hand down his boot, gets stuck, and falls over, knocking into me and sending the coins scattering into the grass.

But its fine. Mum helps me scoop them up while the King still fights with the coin now trapped at the bottom of his boot. He doesn't seem to think to take the stupid boot off.

I hope this works.

"Winds of Time take me away. To the day before today. Choose a coin and pay the fee and Father Time will honour thee." The words tumble out so quickly I don't even take a breath.

Please **please please** let it work otherwise Mum will end up as Queen of England and I'll never be born.

Which means I'll never bring the King to 1999 to meet her.

Which means I'll be born.

Which means I *will* bring the King to 1999 to meet mum and then I won't be born again.

I'm sure Timewalkers is never *quite* this confusing.

The storm comes from nowhere; one minute the grass is as soft and fluffy as a green kitten, the next it's flattened as if a herd of wild elephants has chosen it as their favourite picnic spot. The wind tears at my clothes and hair, lifting me from my feet and throwing me backwards. There's a second, stronger gust and my feet drag against the grass, pulling me along like a piece of paper.

I don't close my eyes this time and focus on the canal. I watch as it's dismantled, piece by piece.

People come and go so fast I can't see them but I see it turn back to a muddy trench and then into fields. The moon and sun chase each other through the sky until I feel dizzy, and I have to close my eyes in the end.

I wait until the wind drops before I open them again.

I'm in the woods now. There's a ladybird climbing over my hand. I watch it navigate my fingers before I sit up.

The King is lying in the bracken beside me, snoring loudly.

I did it.

I brought the King back to his own time.

Which means it'll be my fault when they chop his head off.

I shake that silly thought away. It's history. History has to stay the same. Even Kings can't change centuries when they feel like it.

"What on earth happened?"

I feel my face do its dead fish impression as Mum sits up slowly, bits of leaf and twig clinging to her jumper. She rubs her eyes and stares around.

Okay. *That* wasn't supposed to happen.

Chapter Thirteen

I Thought It Might Be Something Like That

Mum brushes herself down and gazes around. A terrible thought hits me. What if Grandpa Bill doesn't have any

1999 coins left? What if mum has to live the rest of her life in the seventeenth century?

I check both arms quickly. Am I fading out of existence?

I seem to be as solid as ever. Which must mean history is safe for now. I hope.

"Where are we?" She asks. "What happened to the canal?"

There's no point in lying. She's stuck here now, so I might as well tell her the truth. All of it.

"The canal's not going to be built for ages yet." I tell her. "It's 1645."

I wonder if she'll laugh at me. Or cry. Or just think she's dreaming like I did.

Her clear, almost Mum-but-not-quite eyes stare at me.

"So the canal won't be built for another 134 years?"

She's taking this very well. Plus, how does she know exactly when the canal was built?

She opens her hand and the coin drops out and lands in the grass, sizzling like bacon. I drop mine at the same time.

"Well. I've never gone back as far as the Civil War before. Dad won't let me go back any further than the 1890s. He says its too difficult to get coins before that."

I stare at her.

She knows.

She knows about the time-travel.

"You look like a dead fish when you do that."

I gulp and nod. "You've done this before."

"Oh, loads. It's fun."

It's really not fun.

She glances at the King asleep on his back. If he had normal clothes on he'd look like dad when he watches the rugby.

"So he's the *actual* Charles the first? Figures." Then she transfers her gaze to mine. "Where do you fit in then?"

I don't know what to tell her. All the rules of time-travel from all the stories are just going out of the window. I think I'll bring a pterodactyl back as a pet next time.

"I'm your daughter from 2020. I accidentally went back to 1645 and this Roundhead guy was going to kill the King so Grandpa Bill gave us both coins but he didn't have any for 2020 just 1999 so we came here instead."

I take a breath. She's never going to believe all that.

"Oh." She says, nodding. "I thought it might be something like that. Cool."

Cool.

I tell her I'm her not-yet-born daughter and she just says *cool*?

The King gives a great yell and leaps up, kicking his foot wildly.

"It burns. It burns like the fires of hell!"

He dances around, jiggling his leg until he finally manages to drag his boot off.

"Oh. Right. The coin." I forgot I shoved it down his boot. They get very hot before they disappear. "Well it's your fault. You wouldn't hold it."

"Confound the thing." He pulls his boot back on. "You have brought me back to face my doom girl."

"You can't hide in the future." Although Uncle Tommy is.

Has.

Will.

But Uncle Tommy's not the King. If the King disappears it's going to be noticed.

Mum examines the big, pinky-purple flower growing out of a bush. "So it's, what, September? 1645? Before or after Rowton Moor?"

"After." The King says. She nods. Mum's degree is in history. Or it will be. I never realised how clever she is. I'd never even heard of Rowton Moor. Or the Roundheads. Or the Civil War.

"So the Roundheads have taken Chester. You're supposed to head into Wales."

The King doesn't move. "Does it make any difference if I escape their clutches now or later? Let them murder me today."

"We should go to Carnsew Hall." I suggest. I need to know what happened to Grandpa Bill and Tom.

"Is it still called Carnsew Hall at this point?" Mum strikes out towards where the trees are thinnest. "Well, come on. Time and tide wait for no man."

I catch up with her and the King follows. "How do you know the way?"

She shrugs. "Sydnam Hall is just north of where we were by the canal. Moss and lichen tend to favour the north side of trees, where there's less sunlight. They like it damp."

"My glorious Lilly. I swear you are as clever as any of my advisors."

The King tries to take her hand, but she pulls sharply away.

"Much cleverer probably. And you're married. So get off."

The King is clearly stunned by her attitude. He's probably used to girls falling at his feet.

"But I am the King of England. Appointed by God. Sweet Lilly, whatever you desire, it is yours."

Mum turns and looks at him properly. I know that expression. That's her *don't you play innocent and pretend you pushed your brother in the canal by accident* face.

"You're a rich, over-privileged man who started a war that killed thousands of people all because you couldn't share power with parliament. I preferred you when I thought you were some geeky guy in a costume."

And she heads off, north. Leaving the King as shocked as if she had hit him.

We leave the wood and find the track that will one day be the main road with cars zooming past and flattened squirrels. I keep my eyes to the ground, searching for that coin. What will I do if I don't find it? And what happens if I get back a couple of years too soon? Will there be two of me?

"I've always wanted to see Sydnam Hall as it used to be." Mum says as we walk. "Before the area was built-up and the National Trust installed electricity and running water."

"I *like* electricity and running water. And WiFi."

"What?"

"It's like this super-fast Internet. You have the Internet in 1999 right?"

She sounds insulted. "Of course we do." Then she smiles. "But Dad hasn't cottoned on yet. He won't even buy a computer for the house."

"He will." I assure her. "Though he'll never work out how to use it."

The King, now recovered from the effects of 1999 alcohol and being told off by mum, insists we use the secret tunnel to get into Carnsew Hall, just in case there are any Roundhead soldiers still hanging about.

And he's got a point. General Poyntz won't have given up looking. He doesn't have the sort of face that gives up easily. It might not be safe yet.

The entrance is a little, well-hidden cave beneath the mossy roots of an enormous oak tree.

"Wow." Mum says as we drop down onto a leaf-covered floor. Light filters through the roots that are now above our heads. "I wonder if this tunnel's still there? I'll have to go and look. When I get back."

If she gets back. Though I don't add that.

The tunnel leads down, then up. It's quite narrow and pitch black. Neither mum nor I have anything useful in our pockets, like a torch or a penknife, or a handy portal back to 2020, but the King takes the lead and we feel our way forwards until we reach what feels like a wooden panel.

The King taps on it. It'd be just my luck if General Poyntz had moved in and was staying in the room on the other side. He's probably there now, lying on the bed and doing whatever the 17th century equivalent of playing on his phone is.

Probably reading.

The King taps again and we wait. I don't like being in the complete dark. I feel blind. But finally the wooden panel scrapes open and light floods the tunnel.

"Oh. My goodness."

Anne, eyes wider than even when she saw my Pocket-Pet (which I've left in 1999 so it'll be very dead by 2020) helps us clamber out into the blue bedroom. "Oh my." She says again, curtseying to the King.

"Where is Mistress Carnsew girl? Take me to her." The King brushes himself down. He doesn't look very regal any more, all covered with leaves and soil, but at least he's not still drunk.

Anne looks terrified. "Oh no Sire. I can't. You can't stay, any of you." Then she looks at me with terrified rabbit-eyes. "Especially not you Miss. Everyone's heard the story of your witchcraft. It's said you did sweep the King into the air on your broomstick miss."

I want to laugh, but it feels very serious.

"Where's Gertrude?"

"Downstairs." Then she pauses. "With her husband-to-be miss. I daren't disturb them."

"Husband to be? She's already married."

To a man living happily three-hundred and fifty years in the future. So it's not much of a marriage. But still.

"Who's she marrying?"

Anne's face collapses and she starts to cry.

"General Poyntz miss." She says.

Chapter Fourteen

Watch For the Witch

Anne sits on the bed and covers

her face with her hands, sobbing.

"He had Master Tom prisoner you see. And

William Tremayne. Swore he'd kill them both if

the Mistress didn't agree to marry him. He's

always wanted Carnsew Hall. Said he's a mind to change its name."

"To Sydnam Hall." I finish the sentence for her. That's his first name, Sydnam.

She nods and sniffs. I sit beside her on the bed.

"Where're Grandpa Bill and Tom now?"

"Here." She sniffs again, "In the cellar. He's threatening them something awful miss. He wants them executed as traitors."

"What do we do?" I ask the room. I like Gertrude. She doesn't deserve to have to marry that horrible man.

"Mistress Carnsew needs must marry again." The King says. He doesn't sound very outraged.

I half turn and glare at him. "Why does she need to marry? She doesn't *need* a husband."

"All women need a husband to protect them. Perhaps Sydnam Poyntz will prove a better husband than a general."

Mum gives a too-obvious snigger. "Sydnam Poyntz was an extremely successful General. He won at Rowton Moor, Parliament gave him a five-hundred pound reward -"

Mum stops when she sees my expression. Right now nobody in this room wants to know anything good about General Poyntz.

I lie back on the bed, trying to keep my eyes away from the big painting of Father Time. I don't want to study it too closely in case I realise it's turned into Grandpa Bill too.

"Can we get Tom and Grandpa Bill out of the cellar?"

"I've tried miss, but General Poyntz keeps a guard there night and day. He warned them to watch for the witch who might return."

"You don't want to be accused of witchcraft." Mum looks worried. "They hanged so many innocent women. Honestly, they were all ridiculously paranoid. Totally believed there were witches everywhere."

The King takes off his hat. The feathers look very battered. "And are we not right to guard ourselves from the evil of witchcraft?"

"It's wasn't witchcraft though. It was usually harmless old biddies who'd upset a neighbour."

"There is evil in every generation."

"Yeah. And the evil people are usually the ones doing the accusing." Mum faces him boldly. Like some sort of heroine in a story fighting injustice. Why have I never seen this side of her before? Why is it all I've ever seen her do is cook dinner, talk about the past, and shout at me?

"I'm surrounded by disobedient women."

"Well, the tunnel's behind you. Feel free to scuttle off and hide."

The King's eyes glint in the sunlight now oozing through the heavy drapes. He slams his fist down onto the dresser so hard the big china bowl shudders. "You would do well to respect your King."

Mum looks about as frightened as she did that parent's evening when Mr. Hodgeman complained Jonathan had been drawing underpants on all the historical figures in the text-book. She looked pretty scary when she made Jonathan research the sort of underwear every single historical figure would have worn though. Who'd have known that Cleopatra's knickers were linen?

"You got drunk and tried to stab a duck. It's hard to respect that."

For a terrible moment I think the King's going to have her executed or something. He could order her death easily back then. I think that's what this war's all about, taking that sort of power away from Kings.

Then he starts to laugh. A great, big belly laugh that rises up through his body even though he's trying to look severe.

"I tried to stab a *duck*?"

She nods, trying not to laugh too.

"And I failed?"

"It got clean away."

All three of us explode in gales of laughter. Anne stares, bewildered, as I roll on the floor about something that won't happen for three hundred and fifty years. And yet it happened today.

As I laugh, my eyes are drawn to the painting on the wall as if it has some sort of power over me. It's like when Jonathan has the TV on and I'm trying to do my homework; my eyes slide to the screen without meaning to. I stubbornly refuse to look at his horrible old face and so focus instead on the hourglass and scythe.

Then a chill touches my spine and runs all the way down like a trickle of ice-cold water. Father Time's cloak, painted in black oils with visible brushmarks, is *moving*. Just as if it's being blown by the wind. I can *see* the heavy fabric flap around his shoulders like a sail on a ship. I blink hard and move forwards. It looks so *real* suddenly, like it's more than just colour on canvas. I feel I could actually join him in the painting.

"Find me some clothing more suitable for a common man." The King commands Anne in a way no common man would ever command. I blink harder and Father Time's cloak looks like oil paint again, not cloth.

The King unbuckles his sword and leather belt and throws them on the bed.

"If I am disguised, I may be able to move freely around this house."

We decide disguises are a good idea. But probably not enough on their own. I wriggle back into a long dress and hide my hair with a little lace cap like Anne wears.

"The General doesn't bother with the servants. I doubt he'll even look at you." Anne helps mum pull on her dress. She looks like she looks when she guides visitors around Sydnam Hall.

No. *Carnsew* Hall. I don't ever want it to be called Sydnam Hall.

Even though it already is in my time.

That's a bit of history I want to change.

Mum examines the painting of Father Time on the wall and I finally let my eyes look at his face. It's a relief to realise it doesn't look like so much like Grandpa Bill any more. Maybe the other one never did. Perhaps I only imagined it.

The painting looks less real now, less as if he might climb out of the picture-frame, with his thin, bony arms and fierce expression.

"How many of Poyntz's soldiers are in the house?"

"Six. Two guarding the cellars, two at the front and two at the back. It's as well you used the secret passage."

Six. Six men. Probably with guns.

"I wish I still had my Pocket-Pet. They were really scared of it." Though I'm not sure the same trick would work six times. They'd have to be really, *really* stupid.

Deciding I still want to wear my jeans under my dress, I pick them up from where I threw them and a handful of gold coins fall out of the pocket and

clatter onto the floor, rolling in all directions.

Anne gives a little gasp.

"Are you so rich you can throw gold sovereigns

away miss?"

I gather them up. "Is that what they are? They're

his. He tried to chuck them in the canal. Are they

worth a lot?"

"One of these would be ten months wages for

me."

That's quite a bit. I hold the heavy sovereign in

my hand. It's dated 1641. Ten months wages.

A thought creeps up on me, like a little mouse nibbling away in the back of my mind. Chewing a mousehole to let a new idea into my brain.

I count out the sovereigns. I have seven of them. But I only need six. I flick one into the air and catch it.

"I'm going to try a little witchcraft." I say.

Chapter Fifteen

He Can't Even Fight A Duck

I creep down the big staircase, quiet as a mouse in slippers. Past the paintings of Gertrude's family. My family I suppose. I recognise the names from Grandpa's family tree. Margaret De Bohun. Sir Thomas Granville. Elizabeth Plantagenet. Each face looks out at me. Each one alive in their own time. It's funny to think all these people helped to make me.

The oldest portraits are at the foot of the staircase. Old Kings of this country, gold-framed on the high walls. It's like a history book. One Jonathan hasn't drawn all over.

I know where the cellars are. In my day they're the gift shop and toilets. But I don't want the cellars quite yet. I cross the gallery and head for the arched doorway, past the carved coat-of-arms, floor-length tapestries and watched by the images of my ancestors.

Then I stop.

I stop because one of the oldest paintings of all stares at me from the very end of the gallery. And it's a face I know very well indeed.

Dressed in deep red with a white-fur collar, Father Time's features glare out at me. Not the Grandpa Bill version, but the other old man. The original one. The one who used to terrify me as a child. I peer closer. Maybe the artist used him as the model. His face is thin and mean with cold eyes beneath heavy eyebrows. There's no name plaque and I don't know enough about costume to put a date to it.

I'm still looking at the portrait when I hear voices behind me and so I slip behind the tapestry that shows men hunting deer.

"If you expect me to marry you, release my son from the cellar."

I recognise Gertrude's voice, and I can hear the swish of her dress as she moves. There are two sets of footsteps I think. I keep as still as I can, barely daring to breathe.

"Your son shall be freed when Carnsew Hall is mine."

"He's a boy."

"He's a traitor. Be grateful he isn't swinging from a rope."

"You're a greedy man Sydnam Poyntz. You can have the house, but let Tom and me go back to my family in Cornwall."

There's a moment of silence. Then Poyntz speaks again.

"Your husband isn't coming back Gertrude." His voice is soft but it doesn't sound very nice. "He's either dead or he's run away. You're a known Royalist. I could confiscate your property. Arrest you." There's another moment of silence. "But I'd really rather marry you."

"Thomas knew you for what you are Sydnam. You fought as a mercenary in Holland for whoever paid the most. You're no gentleman."

"I will be, when I marry you. When I'm lord of a great hall like this. But don't you understand Gertrude? When there is no King, Parliament will have no place for Lords and Earls. Any man, however lowborn, will be able to rise to the highest places in this country."

So that's it.

Poyntz is just an ordinary man living in a time when the country is run by Lords and Dukes. It's not fair really. He'd be much happier in my time.

I wait for their footsteps to disappear before I slip out from behind the tapestry, down the stone steps and to the kitchens.

Two of Poyntz's men are sitting at the big table playing cards and drinking. I watch them quietly for a moment before one gets up to go to for a wee. I don't think people had proper indoor toilets in 1645, so he'll probably go outside.

I kneel down and very carefully roll the first gold sovereign over the stone tiles. It sounds very loud in the silence. The man looks down, sees what it is and catches it before it can even stop rolling. He grins and brings it to his face, examining it with a very greedy look in his eyes.

Carefully I place the other coins in a little pile beside me. I don't *think* they activate unless I'm actually holding one. But the one I shoved down the King's boot worked, so I'm not taking any chances.

"Winds of Time take me away, to the day before today. Choose a coin and pay the fee and Father Time will honour thee."

I whisper the words as loudly as I dare. I only hope the Winds of Time won't dump me somewhere as well. I still don't trust them.

The wind is so sudden the pots and pans that hang on the wall clatter and rattle thunder-loud, the playing-cards scatter like snow and the cups overturn and tumble off the table. My hat flies from my head as I try and stop my skirts billowing around me like a parachute. The fire in the hearth flickers wildly and the man gives a funny little gulp of shock before the winds scoop him up. I actually watch it this time. They come from nowhere, toss him into the air like salad and he disappears, just sort of fades away to nothing.

The wind drops as suddenly as it came. Aside from the scattered playing cards and fallen drinks, the room looks normal again. The man, and the sovereign, have gone though. I locate my cap from the mangle and pull it back on my head.

"You girl. What're you doing over there?"

I jump.

I was so pleased with myself that I forgot about the man who went for a wee. "And where's John?" He looks around. "I was winning. Come on you old goat, come back and finish the game."

I pick up the cups. Anne was right when she said people didn't really notice servants. I place the next sovereign on the table and bend to gather the playing cards. Out of the corner of my eye I see the man notice the coin. I look away, waiting.

I don't have long to wait. He sidles across the floor and snatches it up, studying it with glee as he realises it really is a sovereign.

I say the words the moment it's in his hands. And this time I hold my cap on my head while the Winds of Time do their stuff. I don't feel guilty. They've only gone back a few years. They're not dead.

It's a pity their sovereigns will disintegrate though.

I tiptoe through the kitchen and out into the courtyard. It's easy enough to make the other soldiers in the house pick up the gold coins.

They're all greedy enough to want to keep hold of the little piece of good luck I send their way. The last man guarding the back door disappears to 1638 without a whisper.

I've done it. Six men. The only Roundhead left in the house is General Poyntz now. Triumphant, I slip back up the stairs to the blue bedroom. The others'll be impressed with my complete and total awesomeness, even though the King thought it wasn't a very honourable way to get rid of them.

He can't even fight a duck, so I hope he wasn't suggesting he should have fought them with his sword.

I open the door, grinning like the cat who got the cream – even though our cat never liked cream very much. She liked very smelly cat-food.

"I did it -"

I stop, mid sentence. My happy boast dying in my mouth.

General Poyntz is sitting on the bed, waiting for me.

Chapter Sixteen

But I Never Will Be Again

He's not alone. Anne is standing

beside him looking really

miserable.

"I'm sorry Miss." She whispers. "I really am."

There are tears in her eyes and at once I feel really

sorry for her. "I had to do it."

"As I will soon be master of Carnsew Hall, Anne knows better than to keep secret tunnels and uninvited visitors from me, don't you Anne? I'd hate for her to lose her place here."

I still don't quite understand. I hope I'm not doing my dead fish impression in front of *him*.

"Where are the others?"

"Ah yes. I'm afraid Anne failed to mention the other six soldiers I have guarding this house. You only used your witchcraft on half of them."

He nods at Anne. I realise now she must have told him we were here. "Go back to work now. Good girl."

She bobs a little curtsey and leaves the room.

"I really am sorry miss." She whispers again as she passes me. "He would have hurt my Lady if I didn't."

I stare at General Poyntz and he stares back.

"So, witch. I think this town would enjoy watching you hang. Don't you?"

"I'm not a witch."

"No? You stole the King away on your broomstick."

"What broomstick?" Mum always says I don't know what a broom is, judging by the state of my room.

"And now you've used your magic to send six of my soldiers into the past."

I'm amazed he understands that. Especially when I barely understand it. He laughs.

"You think they wouldn't remember? You sent them back only a few years. Ample time for them to find me and explain the power you have."

I didn't think about that. I just thought they were gone for good. Popped out of existence, but not dead so I didn't have to feel bad. Then I remember the objects Grandpa Bill sent back a thousand years. They caught up too.

Oops. Didn't think that one through, did you Vicky.

Poyntz sits back on the bed.

"Tell me about my future girl?"

I shrug. "I can't." Because I don't know. I'm not Wikipedia. I know Greek mythology and every single episode of Timewalkers. But that's not much use to a guy in 1645.

"But by the year two thousand and twenty, all of this will be in your history books."

I stare at him, completely and utterly dead fish like and not caring. He can't *possibly* know where and when I come from.

He holds out his hand and the light catches the small, silver coin between his thumb and forefinger.

"I found this on the Chester road. I think it might be yours."

My coin! He has my coin.

He closes his hand around it. "If you want it back, you're going to have to answer my questions."

"Where are my friends?"

"They're my guests for now. The King will be sent to London and tried for treason. William Tremayne with him. The boy will become my stepson. The other girl? I haven't decided whether she's a witch too. She certainly has an insulting tongue in her head." That sounds like mum. This new, younger mum.

My head spins. I *need* that coin. It's my only way home. But I can't just leave mum and the King and Anne and Gertrude and Grandpa Bill. I take a deep breath.

"Let them all go." I say. "All of them. And leave Gertrude Carnsew alone."

He laughs. "And why would I do that?"

"Because if you do, I'll tell you *everything* you want to know about the future." Or, more precisely, I'll make a load of stuff up and hope he never finds out.

I can tell he's thinking about this. He flicks the coin up into the air and I leap forwards, meaning to grab it before it lands. But he's too quick and too strong, he grabs my wrist and twists me sideways before catching the coin easily.

"Who wins this war?"

I don't answer until he tightens his grip so much it hurts.

"You do."

"As it should be. God is on our side. What happens to the King?"

I try not to say anything until he forces my arm up behind my back.

Oww!

"I'll tell you if you promise to let them all go."

"You'll tell me or I'll break your arm."

The pain rushes up my shoulder and tears well up in my eyes. I don't want a serious injury when there's no proper medicine. They probably treat a broken arm with leeches or something.

"You cut his head off."

He still doesn't release the pressure.

"So Charles is the final King of England." He sounds really satisfied, as if that was what he really wanted all along.

"No he's not." I'm almost crying. "He's *not* because there's a Charles the second. It doesn't work, what you're trying to do. Not in the end. And we still have a Queen in 2020. Loser." I probably shouldn't have added that last bit. Maybe I can convince him *loser* is a term of respect in the future.

He still doesn't let me go. I can't move, and my arm hurts so badly I just want to go home. I hate this. I want my boring life back.

"So it seems I shall have to have the whole Royal family executed." He decides. "His wife. His children. All of them."

"You can't do that! I mean, you *don't* do that. History says."

"History hasn't been written yet. Now you've warned me, I can change it."

What was it the King said when he read that history book? *My death brings a period of misery to this country. There will be no sport. No theatre.*

No Christmas. All the simple pleasures, stripped from my people.

If Poyntz murders the whole royal family then maybe that misery will never end. No Christmas. That's an unbearable thought. I *like* Christmas. Sport I can give or take, but Dad wouldn't be Dad if he couldn't watch Rugby.

I have to stop him. Any other deaths will be totally my fault.

But I don't know how to stop him. I can't even stop him breaking my arm.

"Tell me more about my future. Tell me that I become a great man of renown. Greater than any Duke or Count. Tell me they place a statue of me in London. Tell me I am loved and admired."

"I don't *know* what happens to you. You're just some guy who lived three hundred and fifty years ago. You not important." Even as I say that, I think I might be wrong. I think everyone's important. Everyone's part of history.

He brings his head close to my ear and hisses like a snake. "Then I will ensure I am remembered. I will burn this house to the ground and Gertrude with it if I have to."

"I thought you wanted to marry her."

"I want what she has." As he says those words and he sounds like a jealous little boy. "I want her family line. I want to point to my ancestors on the wall with pride. I want my portrait to hang next to Kings and nobles. She can do that. Why can't I?"

"So what?" I say crossly, trying not to cry. "Noble blood doesn't mean noble deeds. It's what you *do* that defines you. Not where you come from." That's a line from Timewalkers, season six, episode ten. My favourite episode.

But I don't think he's even listening any more. "I will order the deaths of every Lord, Earl, Count and Duke in the country." He snarls. "But I *will* be remembered."

He flings me onto the bed and snatches up a candle from the dresser. Then he approaches the heavy drapes and brings the flame close to the fabric.

He's *mad.* Seriously, totally bonkers. He doesn't care if he's remembered as a good man or a bad one. He just wants to be remembered. And if I let him murder a load of Dukes and things, his Wikipedia entry will go from *random General in the Civil War* to *mass murderer.*

"I will burn away Gertrude's family history." He promises.

But Gertrude's family history is my family history too.

There's only one thing I can do. I look up into the face of Old Father Time and give a little jolt of surprise.

He doesn't look angry or fierce any more. Suddenly, he looks kind. And sad. Like he knows what I have to do and he's sorry.

The sands in the hourglass have almost run out. Even as I stare at the painting I see the last few grains drop though the narrow glass tube.

The drapes start to smoulder as the flame begins to eat into the fabric. I bet *nothing* in 1645 is treated with flame retardant.

I bet they don't even know what flame retardant *is.* They'd probably think it was witchcraft. This house is all wood timbers. It'll go up like a bonfire.

Carnsew Hall was never burned down. Renamed, but not burned. This is all because of me. I'm changing history. I'm making it worse.

I close my eyes to stop the tears.

And I say the words.

"Winds of Time take me away, to the day before today. Choose a coin and pay the fee, and Father Time will honour thee."

I almost can't say that last line because of the lump in my throat.

The wind fills the room so powerfully I'm thrown backwards in a pile of bedclothes. The window bangs open with such force the glass shatters and the canopy flaps like a huge, angry bat above the bed. On the nightstand the china jug overbalances and smashes onto the floor, even the painting of Father Time swings to and fro.

I don't open my eyes again, not until the rushing wind drops and the room is completely silent.

The sudden gale extinguished the fire, there's nothing but a little smoke left. And no General Poyntz.

General Poyntz was still holding my coin.

Now he's in 2020. Or will be.

But I never will be again.

Chapter Seventeen

The Lady Lilly and I

After sitting in that silent bedroom for a while, staring at the place General Poyntz last stood, I disentangle myself from the bedclothes and pull open the door.

So that's it.

I'm stuck in 1645.

I'll be dead before they even invent the train.

If Grandpa Bill has a coin from the 1990s I could go there, but by the time I caught up with

2020 I'll be a grown up. Caught out of time like Uncle Tommy.

My family wouldn't know me.

I'll never be that little girl again. Never fight with Jonathan. Never do fun things like watching Timewalkers or playing the Nintendo.

That life's gone. It's gone and all I ever called it was boring.

I fight back the tears. My arm still hurts from when General Poyntz twisted it. I wonder what he'll do in 2020? Maybe they'll just think he's mad and lock him up. Or maybe he'll be happy in a world where nobody cares if you're a Duke or not.

Or maybe he'll find a 1645 coin and come back. I look around, as if expecting him to emerge from the shadows.

But he doesn't.

I reach the staircase with all the portraits of my ancestors and I'm glad I stopped General Poyntz burning them. History's too important to burn.

Then I realise I can hear raised voices, and as I descend they grow louder. There's a sort of clashing sound too, metal on metal. It's a sound I recognise. One I've heard recently.

I stop at the top of the stairs overlooking the gallery and peer through the banisters.

The King, sword in hand, is fighting one of the Roundheads. I watch, and it's *amazing*.

It's like a dance, the ballet or something, his movements are so smooth, so graceful. With one arm behind his back he lunges forwards on nimble toes and the Roundhead falls back, barely putting up his own sword up in time to defend himself. A minute or two of observation tells me the King is an impressive swordsman. If he hadn't been drunk the duck wouldn't have stood a chance.

To my total astonishment, on the other side of the gallery, Mum is doing exactly the same thing, driving back one of Poyntz's soldiers into the tapestry with her sword.

How come mum knows how to use a sword? I mean, *properly* use it, like she's been fighting all her life.

What else isn't she telling me? Is she a superhero on her days off?

She has *got* to teach me to do that.

I survey the scene in fascination. I've never watched a proper swordfight before, and as the King drives his opponent towards the staircase with every expert swing of his blade, I see the Roundhead's face.

He's one of the men I sent back into the past.

The one fighting Mum is as well. He was the one who went for a wee.

So the other six men Poyntz told me about, they're the *same* six men, just a bit older. That could be confusing.

One of the doors bursts open and four Roundheads, all armed, come rushing in. I recognise every one of them too. How was I to know they'd come back here when they caught up with themselves?

The King thrusts his sword right through his opponent's arm before spinning around and facing the four new faces without an ounce of fear.

"Two against six?" He cries. "Have at your King then, dogs. The lady Lilly and I will finish you."

Is he…? Is he actually *enjoying* this?

The other four men exchange uncomfortable glances before drawing their swords.

This could be bad. Even mum can't fight a whole load of guys on her own. Unless there's a *lot* more I don't know about her. Right now I feel she could transform into a woolly mammoth and I wouldn't be surprised.

I wish I could go back to 2020 and tell her how amazing she is. And I don't just mean at cooking dinner.

My hand slides to my pocket and I withdraw that final sovereign. The one I never used.

Then I have an idea.

"Hey!" I shout. My voice echoes around the high gallery and sounds really loud. "Catch."

I drop the sovereign, and it lands on the wooden floor right in the centre of the four men, bounces twice, and rolls across the floorboards.

They look at the coin. Then up at me. I give them a little wave.

"Not again." One of them cries, backing away. "I won't be carried away by the witch's enchantments."

The rolling coin comes to rest by one of the men's feet. He was the one I sent furthest back. Fifteen years I think. No wonder he looks so grizzled. He leaps away as if it's fire lapping around his toes.

"God in Heaven protect me from evil." He crashes into one of the others and they tumble to the floor, each trying to scramble over the other to escape.

"Retreat!" He yells, clambering to his feet and heading for the door. "Retreat. We cannot fight time magic with swords."

"We must outrun the witch's spell or we shall all be plunged into the past."

"Run!"

The guy the King stabbed staggers away too, clutching his injured arm. And the one fighting mum actually goes ghost-white, drops his sword and bolts, yelling something about how he doesn't want to fight the battle of Edgehill a third time.

I meet mum's eyes. She winks. "Twelve years of fencing lessons finally came in useful."

The Roundheads fall over each other in their desperation to escape one little coin. I laugh and I can't stop laughing. Because I think if I do stop laughing. I'm going to cry.

Chapter Eighteen

Don't Call Them Dumb

 "Vicky."

Grandpa Bill opens his arms

and I run to him, burying my head in his chest and

hugging him hard with all the hugs I can't give to

Mum and Dad and Jonathan.

Then he hugs mum and kisses her about a million times on the top of her head the way he always used to. I sit on the stairs. My legs feel a bit wobbly.

We did it. We won. Sort of.

Only right now I feel as if I've lost everything.

The King declares mum to be as *great a warrior as any he has ever known* and demands she be given the title *The Dutchess of Kirkbury*, and they both share wine and laugh with Grandpa Bill and Tom. The King raises a glass.

"To time and tide." He says. "May they both be kind to me. But I cannot escape the heavy responsibility and burden of the crown." I lean my head on the wooden banisters and try to stop thinking about home.

"He only kept one coin here you see."

Gertrude lowers herself down and sits beside me, spreading her long skirts out around her. "For the year you come from. Just the one. He thought, if he had more than one it would be too tempting to come and see his family again." She kisses my cheek.

"That was a very brave sacrifice you made for me. Thank you."

I rub a tear away.

"You didn't need to marry him. You don't need to marry anyone."

She nods. "I'm already married."

I look into her face and try to see some sort of family resemblance. But she's a lot of generations away from me.

"I sent Thomas away."

"I wasn't really thinking about Uncle Tommy" Uncle Tommy just seems a bit selfish to me. But then, if you asked me to choose between the modern world and no flushing toilets, I think being able to wee in comfort would win every time.

"No. But I was. I always do." She looks a bit like mum does just before she starts to cry. "I used one of William's coins. I sent him to the future. To be safe. I couldn't bear to lose him in battle." She swallows her tears. "He couldn't have done it himself. Time is in *our* family's blood. Not in his.

Not everyone can speak to the Winds of Time. It's why General Poyntz won't be able to come back."

"But that's not fair. Uncle Tommy's got TV and a car and lots of food and you're stuck in the middle of a war -"

She strokes my face with a kind hand. "I want to know he's safe. And no matter how many wonderful things the future holds, he doesn't have his family. So he can never be truly happy."

She gives a long sigh. "History says he died at Rowton Moor. Alone. Bleeding to death on the grass. Knowing he didn't is enough for me."

I hug Gertrude, which only makes her cry more, and when Anne joins us, I give her an extra big hug too, to show I forgive her.

"If I have to stay in another time, I'd like to stay here, with you." It's not what I'd have chosen, but at least they're family.

"What use do we have for a girl who can't ride a horse or dress herself?"

I look up. Tom stands above me, grinning. I'm about to say something *really* insulting, when he bows to me like he bows to the King.

"If you were to stay, I would be proud to call you my sister. You are magnificent."

He takes my hand and kisses it, and the insult vanishes from my tongue.

"So I can stay with you?" Maybe it won't be quite so bad. Carnsew Hall is a nice house. And I suppose I could learn to ride one of those four-legged grass-chewers they call horses.

Gertrude shakes her head. "No."

"Please. I don't know anyone else. And you're family-"

She takes me by shoulders and smiles. "Oh my dear. You don't understand. I would be honoured to have you live here. But, it's not necessary."

"It is *necessary*. I can't go home." I stand up and catch my feet in the stupid dress, nearly falling over.

"I can't go home ever again. I won't see mum or dad or Jonathan. I wish I hadn't poked around in Grandpa Bill's bedroom. I wish I'd never heard of the Winds of Time."

Grandpa Bill shakes his head sadly. He puts his hand in his doublet and draws out a handful of coins.

"I'm sorry. I didn't ever expect to go back. I have coins from 1999, but no later."

"You are *so* stupid Dad." We all look at mum. "You're not thinking are you? I'm here. *Me*. With Vicky. So I'm going to do this."

She grabs a coin from Grandpa's hand, checks the date, winks at me, and says the words.

The Winds take her away, back to the future, just like she asked, and when they drop and the portraits all stop swinging on the walls and the drapes are still again, she's not there.

She didn't even say goodbye.

"And then, I'll do this."

We all turn round.

Mum is standing in the doorway.

Not mum at twenty, all young and pretty with bright eyes and red cheeks from the adventure, but mum. *My* mum. Wearing one of the costumes she wears when she does the guided tours at Sydnam Hall.

I race to her and fling myself in her arms. She laughs and sounds like her younger self again.

"What did you do?"

"I *waited*, silly. That's all I had to do. I went back to 1999. Lived my life. And waited. But I've had a 1645 coin ready for twenty years. The moment I saw the winds take you away in Grandpa Bill's house, I picked up a few of these." She opens her hand and reveals a pile of 2020 coins, all fresh and silver.

"Then I put this dress on, drove straight over to Sydnam Hall and here I am. The Winds Of Time brought me right to you. They always do. They're very helpful." She winks again. "Especially when you don't call them dumb."

Chapter Nineteen

But He's Not A Person

When I finally arrive home I'm

so tired I fall into bed and sleep as

if I haven't slept for a month. I snuggle under my

2020 duvet, centuries away from Carnsew Hall and

its heavy drapes and candles, and I dream.

I dream that I open my eyes and I'm standing on

the rocks next to a wild, grey sea. The wind and

waves crash down all around, thundering in

my ears as I search the dark horizon for shelter. Icy sea-spray chills me and makes the rocks dangerously slippery. It's a lonely place, there are no trees, no birds. No life at all, just that endless, rhythmic pounding of water on stone.

Then I see a figure moving towards me, his long cloak flapping behind him as he glides over the rocky terrain on soft feet. The hourglass at his belt swings to and fro like a pendulum.

I know who he is at once, I've seen that thin, bent shape before. I try to back away, but there's only rock and sea behind me.

Old Father Time slows his pace and I see what he is clearly, an old man, not angry but tired. He's *so* tired. I don't know how I know that but I do, the same way I know the sun will never rise in this strange place.

He gazes at me with sad, pale eyes under thick brows, lined by his many years looking out over this same sea. Leaning on the scythe he reaches out with those skeletal hands.

"It's so heavy." He says. "So very heavy. Will you carry it for a while?"

Because I want to help, I take his scythe and almost drop it, it's taller than I am and takes all my strength to hold it upright.

His skinny fingers fumble at his belt and he unfastens his hourglass. Leaning forward, he ties it around my waist and I stumble forwards, dragged down by the sudden weight. The sand is all at the top, but as I look, it begins to trickle through.

The old man steps back, straighter now he isn't lugging these stupidly heavy things around.

"Keep the Winds under control or they'll blow over the whole world." He says. "And a scythe keeps the grass the right length. Not too long. Not to short."

Then he turns and walks into the sea before I can stop him. I can't give chase because it takes both arms to keep the rotten scythe from falling over.

I wake suddenly, disturbed by my dream, and check Grandpa Bill's watch. It's stopped again, but there's moonlight gleaming through the gap in the curtains and the house is still.

Climbing out of bed I help myself to a glass of water and sit on the sofa in the semi-dark. That was a horrible dream, but it was just a dream. Just my head making up TV shows to keep me entertained at night.

Frankly though, I think my head's had enough entertainment for a while.

A gentle breeze blows the curtain, and for a moment, the moonlight illuminates the whole, familiar room in its soft, silver light. It dances off the books on the shelves, the plants with their long tendrils and the painting propped up by the fireplace.

I drop my water.

The painting. The one of Father Time. It's *here*.

Why has mum brought that *thing* back from Grandpa Bill's? She promised to get rid of it. But here it is, staring at me.

The image is exactly like my dream though, every point of every rock is the same. I brush the worst of the water from my nightie and move towards it. The sea looks so wild, I can even feel the spray, and the cloak seems to move as the old man gazes out into the world.

I remember how heavy his scythe and hourglass are, my arms still ache from carrying them in my dream.

Then I realise he doesn't have an hourglass or a scythe any more. They're gone. His clawed hands hang loosely at his sides now.

I look closer. This is impossible.

The whole painting seems alive tonight, and as I gaze into his pale eyes, they begin to change again. His features shift, becoming younger, smaller, the fierce eyebrows thinner, the hair darker beneath the cloak.

As I watch, the scythe and hourglass re-appear, not all at once, but slowly. As if I'm observing them being painted and repainted.

I stare at this transformation in frozen horror until the figure now clutching the scythe and looking miserably out to sea isn't anything like Grandpa Bill any more.

He isn't even a *he* any more.

I scream.

I scream so loudly I feel like they'll hear me all the way back in 1645. I don't move, I can't tear my eyes away from the painting, but I scream and scream until the light flicks on and mum wraps her arms around me.

"It's okay." she says. "Really. Look away. I never like to look too long either."

I stare into her eyes.

"It – changed. Again."

"I know. It does that. It's always moving and changing. It's *time* you see. And time has to move. Or it isn't time any more."

I swallow and let her guide me back to the sofa.

"But – it *changed* – I saw it." I glance back, it looks different now. "But it was. It was *me*." I say. "In the painting. Holding the scythe. Just like in my dream. Me."

Dad opens the door and staggers in, bleary-eyed from being woken up.

"Everything okay?"

"Fine sweetheart. Go back to bed."

Dad turns round, grateful he doesn't have to comfort a screaming child or clean up sick.

Mum holds me so tightly I can hear her heartbeat.

"Don't be scared." She whispers. "It's in your **blood**. It's who you are."

"Grandpa Bill said that too. But I don't understand."

"Vicky darling. The Winds of Time only listen to Old Father Time."

"No they don't. They listen to me. And you. And Grandpa Bill."

She has this really knowing look. Like when I'm opening a Christmas present and she knows exactly what it is and how much I'm going to love it.

"The winds only listen to Father Time." she says again.

"But he's not a *person*." Why do people keep saying that?

"He *is* a person Vicky. Or he was." She kisses me again and then stands up and looks out of the window through the gap in the curtains. The moon reflects her eyes.

"He's your direct ancestor Vicky. In fact, our whole family line descends from him."

Chapter Twenty

She Did What?

"It's still called Sydnam Hall.

Why is it still called Sydnam

Hall?"

Mum and I stand in the courtyard at Sydnam Hall and stare up at the big doors. It's early, and not open to the public yet, just the staff.

"After Thomas Carnsew died his family had nothing left so went back to Cornwall. Sydnam Poyntz bought the Hall with the money Parliament gifted him. He always wanted to be a Lord."

Then she looks at me with a grown-up expression. "Though it's easier to buy a house than a title."

She kisses me and hitches her bag onto her shoulder. "I met your Dad here by the way." She tells me. She's never told me this story before. Or she might have done, I just didn't listen. "He took a student job for the summer. Dressed up as King

Charles the first for a Civil War re-enactment. How could I resist?"

I laugh as I try to imagine my dad dressed up like the King. He looks better in jeans and his rugby-shirt.

She winks and heads for the doors. Then turns back. "Timewalkers tonight?"

I grin. "Timewalkers."

"Show me the new series. I never seem to the time to watch it." And we both laugh at that as she disappears into work.

Nobody minds me sneaking into the hall before it's officially open. Most of the staff know me, but I still wait until I'm completely alone before I duck under the rope and head for the blue bedroom. The portraits on the stairs are like old friends now, and I pause by one of Gertrude looking very beautiful in her green dress. I'm sorry she never saw Uncle Tommy again.

I push open the door and peer into the room. It hasn't changed a lot, except for the visitor plaque that claims King Charles 1st once slept here. Well, he once hid in here anyway.

I look for a moment at the painting of Father Time on the wall and this time I'm not afraid of him. He seems happier now, not as tired or as fierce. I don't blame him for being tired. I think holding back the Winds of Time is an exhausting responsibility.

But he's got help now.

He's got me.

I cross the ancient carpet and examine the wooden panels. Which one did Anne press to open the secret passage?

I spot the carved rose now half hidden behind a wardrobe that wasn't here in 1645, and I squeeze my arm behind it and press hard.

Something clicks and I hear a grinding, squeaking sound from the wall. Then it stops.

I suppose it's been a long time since the panel last opened, it's stiff with age, so I rest my shoulder against it and shove as hard as I can. It squeaks open about halfway, letting light flood into the passage beyond.

I lean in.

"I know you're there." I whisper. Where else would he go?

Silence.

"History hasn't changed. This hall is still named after you."

Still silence.

"Which means you don't stay in 2020. You go home."

Something shifts in the shadows and I climb in, squinting in the dark. It feels like only yesterday I hid in here with mum and the King.

Someone grabs me around the neck and pushes me against the wall.

"This place full of witches." Poyntz glares into my face. "There are monsters on great wheels outside belching fire. And lanterns light up with no more than a touch. And screens show images from far away, as clear as if through a window. What sort of world is this?"

He's scared.

Not just a bit scared, but *terrified*.

"It's the future. Nothing you've seen is witchcraft. Just science. Just like your ancestors wouldn't know what a gun was."

His grip loosens and he lets me go. I reach into my pocket and take out a folded-up sheet of paper.

"I printed this off the computer last night." I turn it around and offer it to him. "It's your Wikipedia entry. You have a whole page."

His hand trembling, he reaches out and takes the paper from me.

"It's not a lot. But you're still remembered. Even hundreds of years later."

I let him absorb the details before I carry on.

"If you go back, you have to do what history says." I tell him. "Okay? You can't try to kill people or force Gertrude Carnsew to marry you. If you want Carnsew Hall, buy it. Parliament's going to give you five hundred quid. Use that. She's going back to Cornwall anyway."

His mean little eyes look less mean.

"You'd send me back?"

"Yes."

I draw the last of the 1645 coins out of my pocket. A shilling. I had to go through the whole box to find this. I hold it between my thumb and forefinger, turning it around so the poor light hits the image of the long-dead King.

He tries to touch it, but I pull it back just like he did with mine.

"Ah ha. No. You have to *promise* to leave Gertrude and Tom Carnsew alone."

His face collapses on itself, his little beard sags on his chin. He's more desperate to get home than I am. I carry on until I'm sure I've made my point.

"I can't stop the Civil War and save the King. But if I wake up one morning and the history books have all changed." I lean towards him with my best threatening face. I worked on it in the mirror last night. I think it's pretty good. "- Then one day, you'll find a little coin in your pocket. And that coin will send you right back here. Or somewhere worse."

The 1970s were worse, right? All those gross fashions. "And you'll never go home again. Not ever."

It takes him quite a few seconds to agree to my terms. But when he nods. I know he'll do exactly what I say

He won't mess with Father Time again.

Pleased with myself, I jog back down the staircase, through the gallery and out into the sunshine. Mum already has a group of American visitors gathered in a group, their guide-books in hand, cameras clicking as they snap pictures of everything, filling their phones with tiny moments of frozen time.

Mum sees me and winks. For once I slow down to listen to her presentation. Usually I switch off when she waffles on about the past. But not today.

I notice a lone guidebook by the stone urn with the lion's head; I like the glossy pictures so I pick it up.

"So." Mum begins. "Carnsew Hall. An excellent example of late Tudor architecture, if you'll note the casement windows."

I stare at the book.

Carnsew Hall.

It was Sydnam Hall five minutes ago. It's *always* been Sydnam Hall.

I look up, Mum catches my eye and raises her voice so I can hear every word.

"The Carnsew Family lived here during the Civil War. Thomas Carnsew was tragically killed in the Battle of Rowton Heath and his wife and son were left with no money. Their only option was to sell the house. However..."

I strain my ears to hear the next part of the story.

"A Roundhead General, Sydnam Poyntz, bought the house himself and gifted it to Gertrude Carnsew. Nobody ever knew why, although he was rumoured to have been great friends with Thomas Carnsew before they found themselves on opposite sides in the war. Five years later Poyntz left for the West Indies and never returned to Britain. In honour of General Poyntz' kindness, Gertrude

Carnsew commissioned a portrait of him, and had it hung in the gallery with the family portraits."

She did *what*?

I race back inside and look up at all the familiar faces lining the walls. Sure enough, there he is. General Sydnam Poyntz, hanging beside a grown-up Tom just like he's family. I can't help being pleased.

He took his place among the nobles after all.

This is Gertrude's way of telling me everything was all right in the end.

I pause beside the final portrait in the row and Sir William Tremayne, my Grandfather, smiles down from his place in history. Trust him to have the biggest, fanciest portrait of all. Show off.

I grin at the portrait, turn, and run back outside. There's a fantastic play area in the gardens and in a year or two I'll be too old to enjoy it.

Time and tide wait for no man after all.

End

Printed in Great Britain
by Amazon